MARY ROBERTS
RINEHART

MORE WILDSIDE CLASSICS

MARY ROBERTS RINEHART

Mistress of Mystery

by
Frances H. Bachelder

WILDSIDE PRESS

Copyright © 1993 by Frances H. Bachelder

MARY ROBERTS RINEHART

This edition published in 2006 by Wildside Press, LLC.
www.wildsidepress.com

CONTENTS

DEDICATION:

For my husband,
Dr. Stan

PREFACE

As a teenager, I had not yet read Mary Roberts Rinehart's novels but was aware that my parents considered her one of their favorite mystery writers, as did millions of others. When I finally delved into *The Swimming Pool*, the first book I read in the series presented here, it kept me awake for several nights. The initial shock of encountering ghosts in creepy old houses soon subsided, however, and excitement took its place. The temptation to jump ahead and scan final chapters diminished as I began to recognize in the stories a pattern that enabled me to settle down to some excellent entertainment.

But reading a Rinehart mystery is more than excellent entertainment. It is a ride on a literary roller coaster, complete with the prickle of anticipation, the thrill of long slides downward and abrupt climbs up, the jolt of unexpected twists and turns, and the breathlessness of plunging into the unknown. And with Rinehart's mysteries, there's no stopping in the middle of the ride; they hold you fast until the circle is complete.

Many individuals have assisted me in this project. I should like to thank all of them, especially the following: Nancy C. Assaf, Librarian at the Scripps Ranch Branch of the San Diego Library; John G. Vanderby, Librarian at the East San Diego Branch; Laura Nagy, copy editor; my husband, Dr. Stan, and my sister, Myrtle C. Bachelder, for their many helpful suggestions. Finally, my gratitude goes to Dr. Dale F. Salwak for his help in the preparation of this book.

—Frances H. Bachelder
San Diego, California
22 February 1993

CHRONOLOGY

1876   Mary Ella Roberts born 12 August at Pittsburgh, Pennsylvania.

1893   Graduates from high school.

1896   Graduates from Pittsburgh Training School for Nurses.

1896   Marries Dr. Stanley Marshall Rinehart, by whom she had three sons.

1903   First story published in *Munsey's Magazine*.

1908   First book, *The Circular Staircase*, published.

1909   A British edition of *The Circular Staircase* is published.

1913   *The Case of Jennie Brice* appears.

1915   Becomes a war correspondent.

1919   British edition of *The Case of Jennie Brice* is published.

1925   *The Red Lamp* (published as *The Mystery Lamp* in Britain) is released.

1927   *Lost Ecstasy* (published as *I Take This Woman* in Britain) appears.

1930   Publication of *The Door*.

1932   Stanley Rinehart dies.

1940   *The Great Mistake* is published.

1941   British edition of *The Great Mistake* released.

1942   *The Haunted Lady* published.

1945   Publication of *The Yellow Room*.

1948 *A Light in the Window* is published.

1949 A British edition of *The Yellow Room* is released.

1952 *The Swimming Pool* (published as *The Pool* in Britain) is released.

1953 Receives Mystery Writers of America Special Edgar Award.

1958 Mary Roberts Rinehart dies on 22 September, aged 82 years.

I.

THE CIRCULAR STAIRCASE
(1908)

THE STORY

Sunnyside: What could be a more inviting name for a summer home? The property, which appears to be as cheerful as its appellation, shows no evidence of what is ahead for the new occupants. But one thing does seem a little odd to Rachel: she learns that the housekeeper, who has been left in charge while the owners are away, has recently moved out of the house and into the gardener's lodge.

The large, Elizabethan-style home, within driving distance of town, is situated on a hill overlooking a great expanse of green lawn and hedges. A typical summer residence, although on a larger scale, it does not have a cozy atmosphere, especially on the first floor. Partitions have been replaced with columns and arches, giving the effect of coolness and space, but allowing voices to echo uncomfortably. Even though the place is well-lighted, sudden reflections from the mirrors and polished floors give Rachel and Liddy a sense of uneasiness as they inspect the area.

The house is rectangular in shape, with the main door located in the middle of the long side. In the east wing in sequence are the living room, drawing room, billiard room, and finally a den or card-room with a little hall opening onto the porch.

From the hall a narrow circular staircase winds its way up to the second-floor bedrooms and dressing rooms. The rest of the house consists of a kitchen, breakfast room, dining room, corridors, and three rooms in the west wing of the basement. Altogether there are twenty-two rooms and five baths.

Although somewhat isolated, under normal circumstances there could not be a more beautiful or peaceful environment in which to spend the summer months. The trimmed hedges extend all the way to the road, while across the valley—perhaps two miles away—stands the Greenwood Club House, a private club established by some well-to-do men from the city.

Miss Rachel Innes is unmarried, middle-aged, and until now has been perfectly satisfied to spend her summers in the city. When her brother died thirteen years ago, the responsibilities of caring for his two children were suddenly left to her, and Rachel carried out the duties of motherhood in the best way she knew how. When her niece, Gertrude, "got past the hair-ribbon stage," and her nephew, Halsey, "put on long trousers," Rachel sent them away to boarding school. As Halsey and Gertrude grexw older, they spent much of their vacation time with friends. But now that they have completed their schooling and are home again to stay, the three of them decide to take a country home for the summer.

Paul Armstrong, owner of Sunnyside and president of the Traders' Bank, has gone out west with his wife (the second Mrs. Armstrong), his stepdaughter, Louise, and a Dr. Walker, the family physician. While the family is away, Rachel, Gertrude, and Halsey move into the house along with Liddy Allen, Rachel's companion. The first night at Sunnyside is a quiet one. But the serenity ends quickly. For the rest of the summer Rachel will never "put [her] head on [her] pillow, with any assurance how long it [will] be there."

The next morning, one by one, members of the household staff offer various excuses for leaving, so that by noon on the following day Rachel, Liddy, Gertrude, and Halsey are the only ones left to take care of the huge house. Liddy wants to return to the city, but the Armstrong's butler, Thomas, currently a waiter at the Greenwood Club, agrees to come back to Sunnyside providing he is well paid and allowed to sleep in the lodge. He explains that there have been "goin's-on here this las' few months as ain't natchal."

That evening, when Rachel and Liddy are making certain all the doors and windows are secure, suddenly the lights go out. It is then that they notice someone peering in the window, but as Rachel looks, the figure moves swiftly across the porch and disappears. At this early point in the story, the author actually hints at the woman's identity when Rachel says to Liddy, "It's only a woman, maybe a maid of the Armstrongs." But can the reader be sure?

Liddy is so nervous and frightened that Rachel permits her to sleep in Rachel's dressing room. A little after midnight, Rachel hears a rattling metallic noise that echoes along the empty halls, like something rolling down the stairs that lead to the cardroom.

When daylight finally comes, Rachel decides to do some sleuthing in the east wing. She finds scratches on the stairs, and on the fifth step, a round dent. If there had been a burglar, she wonders how he escaped, as no doors or windows have been tampered with. Liddy finds half of a cuff link in a hamper that blocks the east wing stairs.

In the afternoon a fresh supply of servants arrives by cab from the town of Casanova. Anne Watson, who previously had worked at

Sunnyside as the Armstrongs' housekeeper, applies for the position vacated by Rachel's housekeeper and is accepted.

After dinner, Rachel asks Thomas if he has ever seen the cuff link before. He denies it. He tells her that he is sure something is going to happen, however, as at three A.M. the hall clock had stopped for the first time in fifteen years; the last time the old clock halted was when Paul Armstrong's first wife died.

Gertrude and Halsey soon arrive with a guest, John (Jack) Bailey, cashier of the Traders' Bank. He is tall, good-looking, tanned, around thirty, and has a small mustache. She also notices his direct gaze, which she likes. As the narrator of this story, Rachel says, "I am particular about Mr. Bailey, because he was a prominent figure in what happened later."

It is Saturday night. Rachel goes up to bed, leaving Halsey and Bailey in the billiard room. At the fateful hour of three A.M., in keeping with Thomas's prediction, the quiet of the house is broken by a single revolver shot. In the hall, at the foot of the circular staircase, Gertrude and Rachel discover the body of a man Rachel has never seen before. Halsey and Bailey are nowhere to be found.

The dead man is later identified as Arnold Armstrong, son of Paul Armstrong by his first marriage. It turns out that Jack Bailey knew Arnold and the two did not get along. Arnold had been in trouble last spring—something to do with the bank.

Quite naturally the question arises as to whether Bailey is guilty of shooting Arnold Armstrong, but neither Gertrude nor Halsey is above suspicion either. Where are Halsey and Bailey? Why does Gertrude turn pale when Rachel shows her the cuff link? Why does Mrs. Watson, who is very upset, claim she injured her hand when she fell down the stairs? Liddy finds a golf club on the lawn. Could this have been the object that was heard on the stairs the night preceding the murder?

Rachel takes it upon herself to find the answers and quickly comes across a revolver almost completely buried in the ground. Upon inspection, she recognizes it as Halsey's and decides to keep the gun and golf club in a safe place until necessary to exhibit them. Now she has three clues, or so she thinks. When she checks the box in which the cuff link is hidden, she is horrified to find it empty. The cuff link is gone.

In the process of investigating, Jamieson, one of the detectives assigned to the case, finds part of a letter among Arnold's personal things left at the Greenwood Club House. Although partially effaced, some key phrases are still legible: "...by altering the plans for...rooms may be possible. The best way, in my opinion, would be to...plan for...in one of the...rooms...chimney." For the time being, the words make no sense, but they will prove very significant later.

The story continues to move at a rapid pace as one strange event follows another. Jamieson discovers someone hiding on the staircase and chases the figure into a closet, thinking he has trapped the murderer. But in the closet is a clothes chute and the mysterious intruder escapes.

Rinehart's mysteries would not be complete unless one of the characters collides with someone in the dark, a device she establishes in this novel. As Rachel is hurrying down the drive to find Warner, the chauffeur, she runs into Gertrude, surprising both of them. Rachel notices that Gertrude is limping and an overwhelming thought passes through her mind. Was it Gertrude who ran from Jamieson and fell down the chute? Upset by such an idea, she hurries on and when approaching the lodge, she has a second collision—this time with a man wearing a long coat, and a cap with a visor. In an instant he is gone.

Thomas's warning about "goin's-on as ain't natchal" proves uncomfortably correct; such events become so frequent that Rachel fears she will have a nervous collapse. So it is with much relief that she recognizes the familiar purring of her car as it nears the house. Halsey has come home but cannot tell Rachel where he has been.

Tuesday evening is quiet, the calm before a storm. Then suddenly the tumult hits with full force. Halsey reads in the paper that the Traders' Bank has closed and Jack Bailey has been arrested. It is discovered that securities worth over a million dollars are missing. A telegram is sent to Paul Armstrong, president of the bank, requesting that he return, but the response is from Dr. Walker: Armstrong is very ill, the doctor claims, and cannot travel.

Halsey and Gertrude tell Rachel that Bailey is innocent of all that has occurred. Halsey believes Paul Armstrong robbed his own bank of a million dollars and that he will never return.

The storm does not abate: a telephone call delivers the news that Paul Armstrong has died. Gertrude, who at this point reveals her love for Bailey, is very upset when she realizes that Armstrong is the only one who could have cleared Bailey. Armstrong's stepdaughter, Louise, returns from California, but nobody knows why, and it quickly becomes clear that she has not been told of the two deaths.

The papers are full of news about the bank: interest is high again because of Armstrong's death. Meanwhile, Jack Bailey is released on bail. The astute reader suspects that Halsey is up to something when he tells Rachel he knows just the man to replace the gardener, who has left to go to the club. When the fellow arrives, she is favorably impressed. Even though his clothing is a trifle seedy-looking, he has a pleasant face, black hair, and blue eyes; his name is Alexander Graham. Here Rachel repeats what she said earlier in the story: "I have been particular about Alex because...he [will play] an important part later." The reader by now may have identified Bailey and Alex as one and the same.

Things do not look good for Bailey because of his business connections with Paul Armstrong. Rachel wants to believe he is innocent, but as yet, too many questions remain unanswered. There is no doubt, however, about Armstrong's guilt. Some of the bonds are discovered, but the money is still missing.

Will Sunnyside ever settle down to the peaceful place it is intended to be? That seems unlikely in light of ensuing events. The rappings and tappings continue, sounds that are muffled and thus difficult to locate. Liddy notices a hole in the trunk room wall and Rachel, always the sleuth, is disappointed not to find a secret room. Meanwhile, Dr. Walker and Mrs. Armstrong arrive from California with her husband's body for the funeral. And the very next evening, Thomas is found dead, but there is no wound. Earlier he had told Warner, the chauffeur, about seeing a ghost who was undoubtedly Paul Armstrong. Rachel and Detective Jamieson conclude that Thomas, who had a bad heart, was frightened to death.

With Arnold Armstrong's murder still unsolved, Rachel is determined to stay at Sunnyside until matters are "at least cleared up." Matters remain muddied, however, in part because the mysterious intruder continues to try to enter the house.

A surprising situation arises when Rachel is invited to join Detective Jamieson, Dr. Stewart, who is an interim physician for Dr. Walker, and Alex for a late night excursion to the Casanova Churchyard, where Paul Armstrong and his son are resting: when one of the heavy coffins is opened, the group can see that the man inside is NOT Paul Armstrong!

In the meantime, Anne Watson is lying near death in the hospital. She asks to see Rachel and relates to her a long, tragic story concerning Lucien, her sister's child, and his father, Aubrey Wallace, alias Arnold Armstrong. There were bitter feelings between Anne Watson and Arnold and she confesses to his murder.

Back at Sunnyside that evening, Rachel, who believes someone has been trying to break into the house in search of a hidden room, finally locates the entryway. She just has time to notice a small portable safe, a table, and a chair when the door locks behind her and she is trapped in the unlighted chimney room. After a time, she hears the sound of voices and people hurrying about. Suddenly the door opens and a man enters, leaving his pursuers behind. In the dark, a cat and mouse game follows between Rachel and the intruder until at last he leaves with his followers in hot pursuit.

Alex manages to free Rachel, and the two are met on the second floor by Jamieson, who directs them to the foot of the circular staircase in the east wing. There on the floor is Paul Armstrong, this time definitely dead; his neck is broken.

Now the whole story unfolds by degrees. Paul Armstrong had lost a fortune and, by looting his own bank, had hoped to retrieve the money. With little effort, he enlisted the help of the unscrupulous Dr. Walker, who was in love with Louise. But Armstrong's plans went awry. Sunnyside had been rented without his knowledge and he was unable to get into the chimney room, where he had hidden over one million dollars in cash and securities.

As to the ghost, it was none other than Jack Bailey, alias Alex, who was certain there was a secret room. In his efforts to find it and thus exonerate himself, he frightened the entire household.

CONFLICTS

Arnold Armstrong is almost as much of a scoundrel as his father. To the crime of forgery, he has also added blackmail; while Anne Watson has been demanding money from him for some time, he has reversed the process and has himself become the blackmailer. The tension between the two reaches its peak one evening when he strikes her with a golf club, seriously cutting her hand. Watson retaliates by shooting and killing him. She later dies of blood poisoning resulting from the cut.

Another conflict Rachel has to deal with is Dr. Walker, who, for obvious reasons, wants her to vacate Sunnyside. However, as she explains to the reader, "the series of catastrophes...taught me one thing, that...I have in me the instinct of the chase" and she refuses to leave. On a more personal level is the conflict with her own family. Rachel wishes her nephew Halsey had taken her "into his confidence throughout the whole affair" that summer. "But," as she says, "young people refuse to profit by the experience of their elders, and sometimes the elders are the ones to suffer."

THEMES

Mary Roberts Rinehart once wrote: "It was a great thrill to me when my first book, *The Circular Staircase*, was hailed as something new in its particular field, in that it was a mystery, plus humor... Yet on the day of publication I took my children and went to a remote farm in the country, so I would not have to read what I expected to be most unpleasant reviews. They were not; they were wonderful."

First published in 1908 and listed as one of her principal works, *The Circular Staircase* is still widely read, even though, by today's standards, it does not compare with the violence and horror we now find in mystery books. But its popularity, spanning a period of more than seventy-five years, should tell us something about the unique talent of the author. Rinehart cleverly sidetracks the reader early in the story when Arnold Armstrong is found murdered. True, this crime is an important element, but it is only one of a series of catastrophes fore-

16

shadowing the gradually emerging central theme: the passion for money. Paul, Arnold's father, has "a besetting evil, the love of money," which is not uncommon; but he is obsessed with wealth for its own sake rather than for what it will buy. His plan to retrieve his lost fortune appears to be a simple one. However, unexpected stumbling blocks upset the conspiracy and the lives of five people are sacrificed.

Sometimes we can feel other people's influence without ever having met them. Paul Armstrong fits into such a category. The reader becomes acquainted with this rascal only vicariously, but the author makes it clear that Armstrong haunts those he left behind more surely than any ghost in the rambling old house.

NARRATIVE SUSPENSE

This novel is self-sustaining as a mystery, but further enriched with romance and humor. Even though the verbal exchanges between Rachel and Liddy sometimes appear to have acid overtones, each one knows she could not get along without the other. Most of the time the banter is light and provides moments of comic relief. For instance, Rachel says:

> When I look back over the months I spent at Sunnyside I wonder that I survived at all. As it is, I show the wear and tear of my harrowing experiences. I have turned very gray—Liddy reminded me of it only yesterday, by saying that a little bluing in the rinse water would make my hair silvery instead of a yellowish white. I hate to be reminded of unpleasant things and I snapped her off. "No," I said sharply, "I'm not going to use bluing at my time of life, or starch either."

And after a particularly ghostly evening, the following exchange occurs between Rachel and Liddy:

> "Get up," I said, "if you don't want to be murdered in your bed."
> "Where?, How?" she yelled vociferously, and jumped up.
> We got to the door somehow and Liddy held a brass andiron, which it was all she could do to lift, let alone brain anybody with. I listened and, hearing nothing, opened the door a little and peered into the hall...Liddy squealed and drew me back again, and as the door slammed the mirror I had placed on the tran-

som came down and hit her on the head. That completed our demoralization. It was some time before I
could persuade her she had not been attacked from behind by a burglar, and when she found the mirror
smashed on the floor she wasn't much better.

"There's going to be a death!" she wailed. "Oh,
Miss Rachel, there's going to be a death!"

"There will be," I said grimly, "if you don't keep
quiet, Liddy Allen."

The romantic intervals are provided by Louise and Halsey, and
Gertrude and Bailey. Both affairs are in unstable conditions, but things
do have a way of working out; so Liddy and Rachel, who have returned
to the city, are making plans to attend two weddings in the near future.
In the meantime, the romances have added interest and complexity to a
plot that failed, due largely to Rachel's persistence in seeking a solution.

In spite of all the unpleasant events, Rachel says, "To be perfectly frank, I never really lived until that summer." The circular staircase has led her to new heights of experience.

SYMBOLISM

The title of this novel, *The Circular Staircase*, offers its own symbolic
possibilities: Paul Armstrong's struggle to climb to great heights fails
when, after his final attempt to retrieve the money, he rushes headlong
down the staircase, falls against the door and is killed. When Arnold is
shot and killed, in what more suitable spot could he be found than at the
foot of the circular staircase, a possible symbol of the inward-turning
spiral of dishonesty and criminal intent?

Although experience of their elders could be a symbol for
young people to follow, French poet Charles Baudelaire envisions human beings as walking in "a forest of symbols" that speak to them in
words they do not fully understand. Since experience is oftentimes an
abstract rather than a visual representation, its results may or may not
be apparent. So it is not always a matter of refusing, but more often of
not recognizing the lessons of our elders until it is too late to profit
from them. For example, Rachel feels if Halsey had told her more of
what he knew, it would have been better for all concerned. Halsey,
however, may have believed he was doing the right thing in not being
entirely frank with Rachel.

II.

THE CASE OF JENNIE BRICE
(1913)

THE STORY

It is April. A significant discovery during the annual spring flood, which has again inundated the first floor of her boarding house, reminds Elizabeth Pitman of the time when, in one of the upstairs rooms, a seemingly innocent plot was set in motion. She recalls the events of five years ago, and in an extended flashback the plot unfolds. During that fateful March, the weather bureau warns people that flood waters are rising rapidly. As Elizabeth goes about her house making necessary preparations, she overhears an argument between Ladley and his wife, the actress Jennie Brice, lately of The Liberty Stock Company. Then a third person joins in, a man whose voice Elizabeth does not recognize.

The water continues to rise in the lower hall, finally stopping at the seventh step, where Mrs. Pitman has tied a skiff to a staircase spindle. Shortly after midnight, she is awakened by Mr. Reynolds, another boarder, who tells her that someone has taken her boat. At four-fifteen A.M. she hears the sound of oars in the downstairs hall and discovers Philip Ladley trying to tie up the boat. He explains that Jennie was ill, so he borrowed it to go to the drugstore.

The next morning, Ladley orders breakfast for only himself. When pressed for information about his wife, he angrily announces that she is not there, but will return by Saturday. All at once, Elizabeth's apprehensions surface, and she is now certain that Jennie Brice Ladley has been murdered.

How this firm conclusion enters her mind is difficult to say. Among other things, however, there is the odor of scorching cloth and the sound of quarreling. Then a water-soaked slipper and a broken kitchen knife turn up. Separately, these seem of little importance, but soon the pieces fit together as in a jigsaw puzzle, and Elizabeth thinks she sees the entire picture; it is not a pleasant one.

At 12:30 that afternoon Mr. Holcombe, a retired merchant, rows his boat down the street. Stopping at Elizabeth's front door, he sees a man looking out the window. It is Ladley, who immediately withdraws. Holcombe has spent the morning searching for dogs and cats stranded by the flood. With one oar he poles the boat into the front hall where he finds Peter, Elizabeth's dog, whining from hunger. Just as he is ready to feed Peter, a disheveled Mrs. Pitman arrives and apologizes for having neglected her pet. After a short conversation, Holcombe is preparing to leave when he spots a stained rope end tied to the stair railing. After inspecting it, he informs Elizabeth that it is a blood stain. Glancing at Ladley's door, she tells Holcombe that the rope was new the night before, and she does not know how the blood got on it.

By now Holcombe, certain something is wrong, suggests that they go into the kitchen to talk. There, tired and upset, Elizabeth tells him the whole story, including her suspicions about Ladley murdering his wife Jennie. Holcombe believes that without a body there is no proof of murder, but Elizabeth assures him a body will be found in the parlor when the water recedes. If so, Holcombe wonders, why hasn't Ladley left the house? Elizabeth thinks Ladley is ready to go, but had to retreat when Holcombe came in. At this, Holcombe checks the downstairs hall only to find his boat gone and Ladley's room empty. Holcombe and Pitman peer out the window in time to see Ladley row away from the house and disappear from view. Luckily, the Maguire boys, who live next door, happen to be going by on a raft. Warning Elizabeth not to touch a thing in the room, Holcombe hires the boys' raft and follows Ladley. He returns shortly in his own boat which he discovered at the end of the street where the water stops; Ladley, meanwhile, has vanished.

Holcombe decides to invite Ellis Howell, a newspaper reporter, to work with him on the story. When Howell arrives, Holcombe summarizes events for him, including possible clues he has listed in his notebook. Not until Holcombe mentions the onyx clock missing from the mantel does Howell show any real interest.

Later that afternoon, Elizabeth and Holcombe go to the police station, but there he leaves her. Because the police want facts and Elizabeth and Holcombe are operating only on suspicion, Holcombe is not prepared to talk with them. Although they listen carefully to Elizabeth's story, they pay the most attention when she tells them about the onyx clock.

Elizabeth returns home by boat and as she is about to go up the stairs, she hears someone talking. She is quite certain it is the voice she heard before. However, she finds only Howell with a pretty young visitor whose name is Miss Harvey. Even though Pitman has never seen her, somehow she knows the girl is her sister Alma's daughter Lida, who shares her mother's beauty, but not her arrogance. After recovering from the shock of seeing her niece, Elizabeth asks Howell if he was the Ladley's visitor on Sunday morning; he evades the question. What is clear, however, is that he obviously cares for Lida.

That evening, Elizabeth has a visitor, Temple Hope, the leading lady at the Liberty Theater. A longtime friend of Jennie Brice, she is concerned by the latter's disappearance. Comparing notes, Hope and Elizabeth agree that Ladley may have killed her.

Not long after Hope leaves, Holcombe returns and tells Elizabeth that Ladley has been taken into custody as a suspicious character. Holcombe has decided upon a plan which he hopes will prove a crime has been committed: he will "become" Ladley for a short time, endeavoring to live and think as he did.

The next day, although the water in the house is now very low, nothing unusual is found. Pitman does notice something strange next door, however: Molly Maguire is hanging out a thoroughly drenched fur coat which Elizabeth is positive belonged to Jennie Brice.

Although newspaper coverage of Jennie's disappeance is widespread, there is no assurance she has left the city. Earlier, a young lady resembling Jennie Brice was seen at the railroad station, but since she was with an attentive young man, this did not seem to warrant attention.

A few days after Ladley is arrested, Howell comes to the house to pick up a manuscript for him. He asks Elizabeth if she has found her onyx clock. When she accuses him of knowing something about it, he looks uneasy. Suddenly she is certain he was the man with the Ladleys on that Sunday morning. At first, he jokes about it, but then he asks that she not tell anyone and assures her that he will find her clock. He adds, "There is nothing wrong about my being here...but I don't want it known. Don't spoil a good story, Mrs. Pitman."

By Thursday of the week Jennie disappeared, the police release Ladley, who then returns to the boarding house and requests his old room. Elizabeth agrees but she is not happy about it. Holcombe, however, is delighted, as now he can continue his detective work. He rigs up a periscope to check on Ladley through an opening in the floor. Although it is difficult to hear conversations through the floorboards, when Ladley has a visitor Holcombe does catch a few phrases, among them "Eliza Shaeffer" and "We'll see you through." As soon as the man leaves, Holcombe follows him and finds he is Bronson, business manager at the Liberty Theater.

Until now, Ladley has been *blasé* about the whole affair, but by Sunday Holcombe notices Ladley is upset after reading the morning paper. Holcombe obtains a copy and finds this entry: "Body of woman washed ashore yesterday at Sewickley. Much mutilated by flood debris." That afternoon, Holcombe takes a trip to Sewickley, a Pittsburgh suburb. Returning in the evening, he tells Pitman he believes it is Jennie Brice, but the head is missing.

The case is starting to build against Ladley: Graves, a city detective, arrives with Timothy Senft, a peddler of dishes and tinware along the Monongahela River. Senft recalls helping a man caught in the current early Monday morning. Peering through Holcombe's periscope, he identifies Ladley as the one to whom he threw a rope.

The next morning, Elizabeth sees Molly Maguire brushing the fur coat. Questioning Tommy Maguire, she learns that his father found it across the river on some ice. When the coat is shown to Ladley, he turns pale but denies it belongs to his wife.

That evening Alma's chauffeur brings Elizabeth a note from Lida asking that she visit immediately. Her reason for wanting to see Pitman is to inquire about Jennie Brice, who, she says, is a friend of Howell. Lida claims that Howell has neither called nor visited since Brice's disappearance. In addition, she says her Uncle Jim (Elizabeth Pitman's brother) met Howell walking with some woman across the bridge early Monday morning; Lida thinks it was Jennie Brice.

The next day, Elizabeth goes to the morgue with Graves to view the body, but she is unable to identify it. A scar over the corpse's heart is not helpful because everyone, including Ladley himself, agrees that Jennie Brice had no scar. A Mrs. Murray, mother of Alice Murray, who is also missing, comes to the inquest but indicates that her daughter had no such scar, either. One thing is certain, however: the headless woman had been murdered and thrown into the water. Though the police have no motive, they arrest Ladley again, this time for murder. All they have is circumstantial evidence, but they feel it is worth the gamble to hold him while they investigate further.

Later, an exhausted Ellis Howell arrives at the boarding house and is surprised to learn that Ladley is in jail. "Mrs. Pitman," he says earnestly, "I don't like him any more than you do. But he never killed that woman."

The trial is to take place in May, but meanwhile strange things are happening: the boarding house is filled with a touring company, one of whom, a John Bellows, knew Jennie Brice. When Holcombe hears about this, he stays close to the man and then inexplicably leaves for New York.

One day when Elizabeth is reviewing her list of clues, Eliza Shaeffer, postmistress at a town called Horner, comes to the house. It seems a Mrs. Jane Bellows was a boarder at the Shaeffer farm for about three days. While there, she wrote to Ellis Howell in Pittsburgh and shortly thereafter left and could not be found. When Pitman shows Eliza some pictures of Jennie, she notices a slight resemblance to Mrs. Bellows.

The trial finally opens in May. Elizabeth, one of the first witnesses to be called, is questioned extensively. Damaging evidence is given by Temple Hope when she testifies that Ladley had attacked Miss Brice more than once and that he planned to marry another woman. Now the police have a motive, if the accusation can be proved. According to Jennie Brice's sister from Olean, Jennie was once married to

John Bellows. Strong evidence against Ladley is also provided by Timothy Senft, the Shanty-boat man.

The next two days, many witnesses take the stand. On the third day, Agnes Murray tells the court that Ladley came to her place several times to visit her daughter, Alice. Then on February 28, Alice disappeared, leaving a note about marrying Ladley.

So far, the prosecution has been successful except for actual identification of the body. When the defense begins its case, Jonathan Alexander, a druggist, positively identifies Ladley as the man who bought medicine for his sick wife the night the murder allegedly took place.

Meanwhile, Elizabeth returns home and learns that Holcombe and Howell are back. Holcombe is detaining a witness in his room whom he feels will "sew up" the case. Howell, however, seems dejected: he explains that he has been trying to find the only person who can clear Ladley, but so far has had no luck. The following day, the defense unexpectedly calls Ladley to the stand. Elizabeth has to admit that he makes a cool witness although he is now showing signs of strain. An anxious Ellis Howell is examined and cross-examined but clings to his belief that Jennie Brice was alive Monday morning, March 5. Convinced that she is still living, he has spent two months searching for her.

That afternoon, the prosecution presents a new witness, a Doctor Littlefield, the man Holcombe has brought in from New York. Littlefield remembers a Jennie Ladley asking him to remove the name of "John" tattooed over her heart; he complied, with his assistant as a witness. Any scar remaining could be easily concealed with paraffin, he notes. At last the trial is over, and twenty-four hours later the jury announces its decision: guilty in the first degree.

One evening following the trial, Howell comes to the boarding house. Tomorrow, he says, he will visit the district attorney and make a confession, but first he wants Pitman, Holcombe, and Lida to hear his story. Earlier, Howell relates, Bronson and he presented an idea to the Ladleys, assuring them they would be paid for their part in the scheme, whose gist was faking Jennie's disappearance. Jennie would go to a farm in Horner for a week's vacation. Since her husband had threatened her life a few times, it would be simple, they felt, to make it look as if she had been murdered. The plan called for finding Jennie after that week, thereby establishing Ladley's innocence. The excitement would improve the theater's business and Howell would have a rousing story for his editor. After much arguing, the Ladleys finally agreed to carry out the hoax, which included leaving several false clues around. The onyx clock, as well as the burned pillow slip and broken knife were not on the list. The strategem failed, however, because Jennie could not be found after a week.

Although Howell's story answers some questions, a few disturbing matters have yet to be resolved. For example, what part did the onyx clock and the pillow slip play in the mystery? Who was the girl with Howell walking across the bridge that Monday morning after Jennie disappeared? Who was the headless woman washed ashore at Sewickley?

We find out, as events further unfold, that the girl Howell thought was Jennie was actually Alice Murray dressed to look like her. Alice was living a short distance from Elizabeth's boarding house to be near Ladley, who had promised to marry her. On Monday, March 5, he had planned to travel with her to New York, but the day before—on that fateful Sunday morning—Howell and Bronson had presented their scheme to him. In a later confession, Ladley claimed that all he had in mind was to go along with the plan. But the idea, combined with his hatred of his wife and his affair with Alice, was too great an inducement; that night he strangled Jennie, cut off her head, and put it in a pillow slip with Elizabeth's beautiful onyx clock for a weight.

Now five years later, at the time this story is related, an onyx clock and a piece of pillow case have been found in the river. Now that the flashback is complete and the role of these items is clear, one may wonder if Pitman remains fond of that clock.

SETTING

The setting for *The Case of Jennie Brice* is structured around a physical location in lower Allegheny, an independent city which later became amalgamated into the Pittsburgh metropolitan area. In this low-lying section, Elizabeth Pitman maintains a boarding house. Many of her boarders are theatrical people, as the Pittsburgh theater district is a mere five-minute walk over the bridge from her establishment. Much of the action in chapters eleven through fourteen takes place at the courthouse, where the trial is realistically portrayed. Other settings are the home of Pitman's sister Alma, the Liberty Theater, Molly Maguire's house, and the towns of Sewickley and Horner.

CHARACTERS

Elizabeth Marie Pitman, the viewpoint character in this story, comes from a wealthy Pittsburgh family. When she eloped with Pitman, who has since died, "she sacrificed everything to discover too late that she was only in love with love." After twenty years, she returns to Pittsburgh and buys a house in lower Allegheny which she opens to boarders. At middle age, Elizabeth Pitman is poor, "shabby, prematurely gray."

During the course of the novel Pitman concerns herself with the plight of her niece, Lida Harvey, who is determined to marry Ellis Howell. Howell, a young newspaper man with a college education, is from a good family, but impecunious. Elizabeth Pitman has ambiguous feelings about the liaison, based in part on her own experience. "I am helping the affair along," she says, "and what if it turns out badly?" But she feels the two of them are right for each other, and perhaps—just perhaps—she finds satisfaction in aiding the two as they repel efforts to separate them.

Most of those efforts are coming from the direction of Alma, Lida's mother and Elizabeth Pitman's sister; while she is not prominent in the story, her influence is strong. Described as a beautiful woman, she is also harsh and arrogant. Howell, determined to further his career and be accepted by Alma, works out a plan with Bronson, business manager at a downtown theater. And this is where Philip Ladley and his wife enter the picture.

There is nothing about Philip Ladley that anyone could like. Always dangling a cigarette from his mouth, he is short, fat, and somewhat bald, with a personality devoid of positive qualities. His wife, an actress whose stage name is Jennie Brice, takes care of the bills as he is currently unemployed and wholly uninterested in working, although he claims he to be a playwright. Any scheme to get rich quick appeals to Ladley. Alice Murray, a stenographer, knows nothing of the plan, but is motivated to do as Ladley asks because of his promise to put her on stage and to marry her.

Holcombe, a supporting character who helps Pitman solve the murder, is a retired merchant. A small, elderly gentleman, he seems eccentric, but his speech and actions belie his true make-up. Holcombe has won Pitman's affection; the implication is strong that he will rescue her from a life she herself describes in rather pathetic terms: "I am a lonely woman, and getting old, and I'm tired of watching the gas meter."

CONFLICTS

Rinehart wastes no time involving the reader in the first conflict of the story. The opening line, "We have just had another flood," is an indication that her characters will struggle against the forces of nature. In spite of the difficulties brought on by the flood, this one recalled from five years previously has, in the long run, worked in Pitman's favor. For the Ladleys, however, that flood meant doom. The rising tide of Ladley's rage against his wife engulfs him, and he, too, is destroyed. Even though Ladley contends he never meant to kill Jennie, temptation and weakness are his downfall.

Interwoven throughout the book is another prolonged struggle, although not as serious as the Ladleys', involving the revelation of true identities. It is, nonetheless, upsetting to Elizabeth as she wrestles with an inner problem: twenty years ago when she eloped with Mr. Pitman, she was snubbed by her family and never reconciled. Purely by accident she meets her niece Lida and it becomes a constant struggle to keep from revealing that she is Lida's aunt. In addition, old Isaac, the loyal family servant she once knew so well and whom she has not seen in twenty years, recognizes Pitman. But she tells him he is mistaken. However, her love for Isaac is so strong that she unwittingly reveals her identity by calling him "Ikkie," her baby name for him. Now Isaac must live with his inner turmoil when she makes him promise not to tell. In both cases, Elizabeth's past continues to affect her present. The rejection by her family has affected her life in every way, and even now she is burdened with the necessity of denying her true birthright. Thus, Rinehart's story is elevated beyond a mere murder yarn to incorporate elements of real human pathos.

THEMES

By setting the murder against the backdrop of a boarding house where flood waters slosh against the front door, slip into the hall, and rise slowly up the stairs, Rinehart has tapped into a strong sense of dread, danger, and foreboding. The house is dark and outside the wind is blowing. With the gas shut off, there is a chill in the air which adds to the eerie atmosphere. Although the flood and the dreariness that accompanies it are enough to make Elizabeth uneasy, she senses something more, a disquiet she cannot shake. Evil is afloat on this dark sea: it laps at Pitman's consciousness as surely as the muddy water engulfs her home and threatens her livelihood. One of Rinehart's major themes, human perfidy, is thus mirrored in the picture of a nature running out of control.

Holcombe, a somewhat pompous but likable man, embodies another of Rinehart's themes. He does a good deal of thinking and delights in quoting Herbert Spencer, one of whose theories is that the minds of human beings have advanced from simple animal responses to reasoning processes. Perhaps Holcombe compares himself to Spencer. At any rate, he influences Elizabeth to the extent that she becomes accustomed to "thinking things over and trying to draw conclusions." Thus the ability of the human mind to solve the mysteries that confront us is affirmed.

NARRATIVE SUSPENSE

The Case of Jennie Brice evokes the reader's interest immediately and moves rapidly. Only one-hundred-sixty pages long, the book is just the right size for an evening's entertainment.

Rinehart devotes several short sections to a heart-rending encounter between Elizabeth and old Isaac. This welcome surprise is indeed a bonus, since the reader may well expect only murder and mayhem, with humor and romance included to relieve the tension. Encountering Isaac again is a "curious experience," as Elizabeth calls it, an incident that occurs about halfway through the story, at which point the narrative slows slightly because of the sudden impact of the unexpected. This break in the movement of the murder story serves to heighten tension, infusing increased energy into the narrative line when Rinehart picks it up again.

Rinehart's description of the emotional scenes involving Isaac and Elizabeth is a stirring part of the story. The bond between them is perhaps reminiscent of the love that Uncle Tom in Harriet Beecher Stowe's *Uncle Tom's Cabin* shares with Little Eva: "The friend who knew most of Eva's own imaginings and foreshadowings was her faithful bearer, Tom." When little Eva was near death, Tom "would not sleep in his room, but lay all night in the outer verandah, ready to rouse at every call."

Rinehart also keeps the narrative moving through the romance between Lida and Ellis Howell (who later marry—Rachel attends the wedding). In addition, there are hints that a second wedding may be imminent. And sure enough, in the last chapter, Holcombe tells Elizabeth, "I have never married...and I have missed a great deal out of life." Elizabeth replies, "Perhaps you're better off: if you had married and lost your wife..." At this, Holcombe interrupts to misquote from Tennyson's *In Memoriam*, "It's better to have married and lost than never to have married at all." Eventually, when Holcombe asks Elizabeth to marry him, she says, "I think I shall do it."

Many mysteries are based wholly or in part on reality; disappearance, murder, and mayhem are, unfortunately, an all too common fact of life. Whether the converse is true—that reality can follow the path of fiction—is arguable. A case in point involves Rinehart and Agatha Christie, who certainly had enough imagination to write a legion of novels. In 1926, Christie abruptly vanished for ten days; thirteen years earlier, Rinehart's novel about the disappearance of Jennie Brice had been published. Are there parallels between the Christie incident and Rinehart's plot? If so, are they merely coincidence? Could Agatha Christie have used the same scheme for her own purposes, whatever they may have been? A comparison of basic facts in the real-life and the fictionalized accounts presents some strong similarities:

Jennie Brice/Agatha Christie are both married to a husband who is involved with another woman who works as a stenographer or secretary, a man who visits his mistress at regular intervals. Both women disappear after a quarrel with their spouses, in both cases the police suspect the husband of foul play, and both were discovered to have used, at one point, the name of the mistress. Also in both cases, the disappearance was labelled a hoax or publicity stunt by at least some of the media. But only Christie was found alive.

The debate still continues about the motives behind Christie's disappearance. All we know for certain is that *The Case of Jennie Brice* could have provided Christie with a significant role model.

SYMBOLISM

Much of the symbolism in this novel evokes a strong sense of Elizabeth Pitman's lost heritage. Isaac, who used to drive the family carriage when Elizabeth was a child, is a clear symbol of her happier days. In addition, the onyx clock represents the aristocratic culture into which she was born. Although at times she needs money and could sell the clock, she never does because the sound of its ticking gives her comfort. Since there are few onyx clocks in the flood district, as the owner of such an elegant item she has been able to maintain her pride and the neighbors' respect. So when Holcombe asks where the clock is, she says, "I turned and looked. My onyx clock was gone from the mantelshelf. Perhaps it seems strange, but from the moment I missed that clock my rage at Mr. Ladley increased to a fury. It was all I had had left of my former gentility."

III.

THE RED LAMP
(1925)

THE STORY

June 30, 1924: Samuel Pepys's *Diary*, Bram Stoker's *Dracula*, and Robert Louis Stevenson's *Dr. Jekyll and Mr. Hyde*—what do these have in common with Rinehart's mystery of *The Red Lamp*? More than first meets the eye. For one thing, William A. Porter, A.B., M.A., Ph.D., Litt.D., makes use of Pepys's rhetorical device to tell a story extending from June 16 through September 10, 1922. But more about that later.

Professor Porter's introduction to his journal is written two years after a strange series of events that occurred at a place called Twin Hollows. The Oakville drama is so called because the thirty-two acre estate is located on the bay three miles from Oakville. Realizing that many people have remained interested in the drama's final outcome, a *dénouement* which the newspapers never disclosed, and believing it a duty to himself as well as to the University to "research" the question, Porter decides to complete the story.

On the night of September 10, 1922, two years earlier, the summer's dramatic events culminated in the main house at Twin Hollows, a large beautiful home once occupied by Horace Porter, William Porter's uncle. Uncle Horace is remembered by his nephew as a small old gentleman with a sharp dry asthmatic cough for which herbal cigarettes provided some relief. Whether his sudden death was actually due to cardiac asthma is questionable. Thus Porter finds himself attempting to solve many other questions that arise during the busy (but far from peaceful) summer of 1924: strange phenomena leave him and his wife, Jane, only half-convinced of what they experience. As Porter observes in his journal, "All houses in which men have lived and suffered and died are haunted houses." While Porter makes every attempt to tell "what happened," he is unsure of the explanations.

We are taken via flashback to June 16, 1922. Commencement week is over. Only eight members of the class of 1870 march onto the field on Class Day. Uncle Horace is missing, but Jane is sure she sees him as she snaps her usual pictures of the alumni procession. When the film is developed, there is without question a ninth figure in shadowy form. Lear, a colleague of Professor Porter, calls it a double exposure and suggests that he show it to Cameron, a member of the Society for Psychical Research and Exchange Professor of Physics at the University, known as "Spooks" to his students.

Several times Jane has surprised her husband with her apparent faculty for clairvoyance; for example, one day she "sees" Uncle Horace lying dead on the floor of the library at Twin Hollows, and a call from Annie Cochran, a servant at the big house, confirms Jane's vision.

With the long summer ahead, William Porter wonders what he has to look forward to. He finally decides that they will spend the three months at Twin Hollows, but Jane, who has always hated the house, refuses to go. Porter attributes her distaste for the place to the fact that Eugenia Riggs, a discredited medium, once lived there. Jane finally agrees to go when Edith, William Porter's niece, who lives with them, becomes so excited about going that Jane finds herself caught up in the girl's enthusiasm. Jock the dog also has some misgivings when they arrive at the old house, and he refuses to enter. That night, however, he moves through it with no concern. Porter wonders if Jock "sees" something that humans cannot.

Thomas, the gardener during Uncle Horace's time, will not go near the house at night—too many strange noises. He is also concerned about a small red lamp in the den: when Annie Cochran found Horace the morning after he died, there were no lights burning except for the red lamp.

Although Jane will not admit to being afraid of the house, Porter, sensing her apprehension, decides it will be better to stay at the Lodge, a small cottage nearby. The main house will be rented. Warren Halliday, who plans to marry Edith some day, will live in the boathouse.

One day, having settled into their routine at the cottage, Porter has a talk with Maggie Morrison, a timid, superstitious farmer's daughter who delivers milk and eggs. He notices that she backs and turns her truck by the Lodge instead of circling around the main house. When asked if she is afraid in the daytime, Maggie replies that she dislikes any place where there has been a death.

Jane has adopted a calmer attitude, but, like Maggie Morrison, she stays as far away from the big house as possible. Then one evening she decides she is behaving foolishly and suggests to her husband that they go to the house and use the red lamp there to develop some pictures. Everything is going well when suddenly Jane feels a cold wind and a few minutes later, she faints. Revived, she contends that she has just seen Uncle Horace. William has his doubts about this, but has to admit his wife saw something.

That same red lamp has proved troublesome to the country people. Six sheep owned by a farmer named Nylie are stabbed in the jugular vein and laid out in a row; Nylie claims he saw the "evil glow" of the light from the house the same night of the slaughter. Later, more sheep are slain in the same manner, and Porter wonders if some religious obsession with symbolistic sacrifices is the answer.

To add to the mystery, whoever killed the sheep left behind the drawing of a triangle in a circle. Questioned by Detective Greenough, a heavyset, pleasant, but shrewd individual, Porter admits he has read about such a symbol in a book on Black Magic. This admission will mean troublesome days ahead for the professor as Greenough tries to build a case against him.

By July, the house is rented to a Simon Bethel, who comes from the west. An ornery, childish old man, he is partially paralyzed and has the use of only one hand. Gordon, his secretary, is a thin boy with a poor complexion and heavily pomaded hair. In response to Gordon's request for a servant, Annie Cochran agrees to resume her former position, but only during the day.

On the evening of July 3, more sheep are killed and the countryside is again filled with terror. Because of the people's superstitions about the red lamp, Porter considers destroying it, but after talking with Annie Cochran, he changes his mind. If the lamp is demolished, she believes the demon in it will be freed. Although Porter feels this is incredible, he locks the red lamp in an attic closet just in case.

Meanwhile, the professor receives an anonymous note warning him that the Lodge is dangerous and advising him to leave. But of course he has no intention of doing so. He decides to take Halliday into his confidence and the two of them proceed to the main house to clean out Uncle Horace's closets before Bethel arrives. While working, they discuss a letter found earlier in the old man's desk drawer. Part of it reads as follows: "I appeal to you to consider the enormity of the idea...If you go on with it...I shall...go to the police...and warn society in general." The words are foreboding but for the moment their meaning remains unclear.

As mysterious events continue to occur, Porter somehow manages to involve himself in the misfortunes and fatalities in a way that makes him appear guilty in the eyes of Detective Greenough. Porter's summer vacation has become a nightmare that worsens with the news of the latest occurrence, which quickly turns out to be a tragedy: Carroway, a recently sworn-in deputy assigned to the sheep episodes, disappears and is believed murdered.

Two days later Simon Bethel moves into the big house and the next night Porter is startled to see a small red light coming from the den window. Then he hears a dry asthmatic cough followed by the odor of Uncle Horace's herbal cigarette. No amount of reasoning helps: the red lamp has again intruded itself into a situation, and yet, how could it? Porter had locked it in the attic and kept the key!

Rinehart continues to tease the reader, this time through the words of Halliday, who is now working steadily to dispel the clouds of guilt thickening over the professor's head. About a third of the way into the story, Halliday introduces the theory that "some curious and perhaps monstrous idea lies behind the sheep-killing, and that it may be the same idea to which the letter refers." At Halliday's suggestion, Porter and Jane set sail on a short trip down the coast with Peter Geiss, an old fisherman, serving as captain. If anything serious happens while they are away, he believes their absence will establish an alibi for the professor. At one A.M., Peter notices that their red lantern on the boat is getting low. As he reaches for the oil can he sees a shadowy figure under the light, but it soon disappears—Uncle Horace again?

Their trip is about to end: Edith wires them that Halliday has been injured. Upon arriving back at the Lodge, they learn that he had given a ride to a man claiming to be a special deputy. When driving along, Halliday somehow lost control of the car. He was found unconscious, but alone. Later, on one of the seat cushions, Porter notices a drawing in chalk—the now familiar triangle in a circle.

From Halliday's description of his accident, it seems he was the victim of an attack which occurred at the same time as the fisherman's vision on the sloop. But the red lamp cannot be blamed for the murder of Carroway, whose body is finally recovered. He had been struck on the head by some instrument and his hands were tied—no supernatural influence there. In the meantime, Halliday and Porter continue to chase clues while Detective Greenough lies in wait, hoping the professor will trip himself.

The strange and often tragic tangle increases in complexity. Maggie Morrison is the next one to disappear and Porter finds Gordon unconscious on the porch of the main house, tied in the same manner Carroway was. He notifies Simon Bethel, who spends most of the time in his room working on a book. During their conversation, Simon tells Porter his infirmity makes him dependent on others, yet the impression he gives is quite the opposite and this makes Porter nervous.

On August 1, the professor writes in his diary that he believes a lunatic may be responsible for all the crimes. Early in the morning, for some unknown reason, the boathouse is set on fire. Reviewing the situation from the very beginning, he is certain that the main house has been the focal point for activity; but now that has changed, as events are occurring elsewhere on the property.

On August 3, Sheriff Benchley takes Greenough off the case and all but Jane feel relief; she is concerned about his leaving them with no protection.

One night as Porter is driving into his garage, he hears a dry cough, senses someone's slow movements, and smells the herbal odor that reminds him of his Uncle Horace. He is startled to come upon Gordon, standing in the moonlight, smoking. He tells the professor that his boss would be furious if he discovers he left the house. Apparently, Simon and his secretary are not getting along. In fact, Gordon is almost a prisoner all day, as Bethel keeps him busy with typing and dictation. Halliday wonders if Simon attacked Gordon; the old man, after all, does have one strong arm. Annie Cochran reports that Bethel seems to be on guard, but against what or whom? He finally admits he is afraid of Gordon and not happy about staying alone in the house.

By August 20 the professor notes in his diary that Simon Bethel has been murdered and both Gordon and Bethel's manuscript are missing. What seems strangest of all is that no relative has come to inquire about Bethel's death. Cameron, the Exchange Professor, had said he had spoken with Simon at one time, but otherwise did not know him other than to suggest him as a tenant. Based on this evidence, Sheriff Benchley suggests that Simon Bethel was not using his true name. Again Halliday reminds Porter that it is an idea, not a criminal, that is involved here.

The house is to be closed for good. Porter notes that "Spooks" Cameron has returned from the Adirondacks and claims illness from an infected hand. When going through his mail, Cameron finds a letter from Bethel written in July informing him of "abnormal conditions" at Twin Hollows. It is possible Cameron will visit the main house to, as he says, verify results of his own experiments.

Almost two weeks after Bethel's murder, the police still have no firm leads. Mrs. Livingstone, an acquaintance of Jane and the professor, suggests that a seance be held in the house; she thinks they might "receive 'a clue, or something,' as she vaguely puts it." Although Porter refuses, Halliday, who is now working with the police, wants to go through with the seance and so preparations begin. Whatever Halliday hopes to find does not materialize during the first two seances and a third is planned; this time Cameron agrees to participate.

Meanwhile, Porter is still suspected because a diary kept by Gordon labels him as an accomplice to Bethel in some unidentified but sinister scheme. Professor Porter is questioned by the police for four hours, during which time he is told that somebody has killed Gordon.

Porter's innocence is finally established when Halliday gives the police information he has put together after working on the case all summer. As the professor writes in his diary on September 7: "Halliday has given me back to life, liberty, and the pursuit of literature." On September 10, the last day of Porter's journal, the third seance is held and the mystery is solved. Halliday's plan has worked: whoever attempted to get into the house during the first two seances is caught during the third. It turns out to be none other than "Spooks" Cameron (alias Simon Bethel), who is found dead at the foot of a ladder. Three times he had returned for his manuscript, which contained incriminating evidence. The book Bethel/Cameron was writing concerned psychic and scientific experiments. He must have realized that the big house was a perfect place to work on his idea, but when presenting the plan to Horace Porter, who was showing an interest in spiritualism, he was met with horror and indignation. His idea, which was actually a "proposal to carry their investigations to the criminal point" so infuriated the old man that he may have died from a heart attack. Of the other deaths we cannot be sure. However, the manuscript contains certain figures which seem to show Cameron experimented more than once during his stay at Twin Hollows. Although he may not have intended to kill his victims, it is possible he pushed them too far into a state of stupor, thereby causing their deaths.

Porter can say in summation only that there are simple explanations for many of the strange happenings during the summer and yet, as the learned professor writes, "We have solved our problem...Quod erat demonstrandum. But there remains still the unsolved factor." He accepts the phenomena but does not explain them.

The ever-present romantic element in Rinehart's stories is more clearly resolved: Edith and Halliday are married. "Love at least is real," Porter observes.

CONFLICTS

In *The Red Lamp* there is a good deal of dissension, but Gordon, Simon Bethel's secretary, is at the center of most of it. Both Porter and Edith dislike Gordon intensely, the latter so much that she nicknames him "Shifty." In addition, Gordon and Simon Bethel go beyond disliking each other; each is afraid of the other. Annie Cochran thinks Gordon feels she is dishonest; thus her immediate reaction is to dislike him. Halliday bases his reasons for not being keen about Gordon partly on Bethel's views of him, and also on the fact that he suspects him of setting fire to the boathouse in an effort to stop Halliday from doing any further work on the case. Gordon hates Halliday because he wishes he were like him, but cannot be. And finally Gordon's hatred extends to the world since he feels he is unable to cope with it. The friction between Gordon and those around him, then, is source of much of the book's conflict.

In addition, Dr. Hayward tells Porter that Uncle Horace apparently had few close friends and that he quarreled with many people. A conflict thus arises between what Porter has wanted to believe about his uncle and the truth about the old man.

THEMES

The main theme is the question of good and evil and finds expression in Cameron/Bethel who is, of course, the culprit in the novel. That he was asocial, had a "reputation as a relentless investigator," and believed in "conscious survival after death" does not make him a madman. If Horace had accepted Cameron's proposal concerning psychic experiments, who knows what the consequences might have been? But it is possible that at the time he approached Uncle Horace, the old man's rejection, the threat of exposure, and the weight of subsequent brooding may have caused Cameron's mind to snap. Sane or not, he committed crimes that took human lives and nearly sent Porter to jail.

The possibility of the existence of a psychic realm is another important theme. Looking back on the summer's episodes, Porter finds he is still an agnostic, whose fundamental beliefs have not been changed by the eerie goings-on at the house. He does realize, however, that there is a difference between Jane's mind and his own and it worries him. She has a unique kind of clairvoyance that troubles Porter's sense of order and sometimes makes her difficult to live with. She is living testimony that prevents him from denying the extrasensory altogether. As he admits in his journal, "Back of everything physical, and greater than anything physical, is the mind. And mind is not an attribute of matter." The power and nature of the mind, he concludes, is often unknowable: "I am now convinced that any attempt to solve these crimes by the discovery of an underlying motive is a mistake. One cannot piece together into a rational whole the fragmentary impulses of a lunatic."

NARRATIVE SUSPENSE

One may wonder if Rinehart's attraction to supernatural material stems from her religious beliefs and doubts. A biographical account notes that "She finally became an Episcopalian, not so much because she believed in God but because she 'was afraid He might exist and must be placated.'" Whatever the stimulus, from her investigation into psychic material Rinehart found that although fraud was evident in approximately ninety-seven percent of the phenomena she studied, about three percent always appeared to be true. She chose to base the story on this three percent, and that choice of topic in itself heightens the book's appeal. Most readers, after all, are intrigued by the supernatural.

If readers are looking for chills, they may be disappointed. The pace here is as ponderous as Porter's thoughts since, in fact, it is through them that the narrative is related. Beginning with Chapter Three, however, after a slow-moving, rambling journey through Porter's journal and its copious citations of authors, poets, and quotations, the story begins to move more rapidly and becomes absorbing. Perhaps Rinehart is trying to clearly establish Porter's thought processes; perhaps she merely errs in including too much detail in the early phases of the book.

Rinehart has said that *The Red Lamp* was probably the most difficult book for her to write. So dissatisfied was she with the first forty thousand words that she burned all she had written and began anew. The slow pace may be a result of Rinehart's own problems in defining narrative voice.

In spite of a slow start, *The Red Lamp* will hold fast the reader interested in psychical phenomena.

TWO HORROR CLASSICS

A reader familiar with Bram Stoker's *Dracula* might well wonder if Rinehart drew upon his ideas when writing *The Red Lamp*; certainly common elements exist. Perhaps the first similarity that comes to mind is the manner of presentation. In *Dracula*, Jonathan Harker tells the story in journal form, as does William Porter in *The Red Lamp*, and both men use shorthand as a writing device. Porter's reason for doing so, however, is not for privacy. Since his profession is English literature, he has always had the desire to write and thus the journal affords him the opportunity. Although both narratives occur under the guise of diaries, each takes on story form—especially *Dracula*—so subtly the reader is hardly aware of it.

As to the story itself, Dracula, who remains in his coffin and is never seen in the daytime, can be likened to Simon Bethel, who stays in his room all day. Dracula and Cameron are also alike in that each becomes active at night—Dracula as a vampire seeking victims to keep himself alive, and Cameron as the "monster" searching for people on whom to experiment. When leaving on nightly excursions, each one exits through a window and travels miles when necessary. Each man uses a characteristic *modus operandi* when putting his prey into a different state or level of existence.

The duality of the Cameron/Bethel character is strongly suggestive of another horror literary classic, *The Strange Case of Dr. Jekyll and Mr. Hyde* by Robert Louis Stevenson. There is no mention in Rinehart's book of Cameron taking a mysterious drug as Dr. Jekyll does in effecting a transformation, but the results of their behavior are similarly violent and tragic. Each man leads a double life characterized by two identities. Whereas Dr. Jekyll disguised as Mr. Hyde commits his acts with no fear of being recognized, Cameron is at times uncertain of his disguise. Even so, as Simon Bethel, a crippled old man dragging one foot, he is consistent in his role, which Porter calls dissociation. So cleverly does Cameron alter his appearance as Bethel that even Gordon, his secretary, probably never suspects him. Feigning paralysis, however, is more difficult. In a weak moment Simon moves his arm and he knows that Gordon has seen him do so. From then on, the two are wary of each other.

SYMBOLISM

The circle enclosing a triangle that Porter jokingly talked about and which got him into trouble with Detective Greenough is an interesting symbol. In simple terms Porter explains it as follows: "The triangle in a circle, drawn around you, will keep off demons." Van Helsing in *Dracula* shares this belief but in a more serious vein: with a crucifix he draws a circle in the snow within which travelers rest free from danger. In a religious sense, the circle represents eternity or immortality and the triangle stands for the law of threes found in all things. The image served Cameron's experiments but included the evil rather than warding it off.

A second central symbol, the small red lamp in the house at Twin Hollows, probably represents not light but psychic phenomena; the color red "was found to offer least disturbance, and was customarily used" when the medium, Mrs. Riggs, lived there. Its blood-colored rays come to stand for the depravity radiating from those who live by its influence.

To William Porter, the Lodge represents peace. The manifestations of peace which he has brought with him are his books, a notebook for his journal, "Jane for solid affection, Edith for the joy of life, and Jock for companionship." Unfortunately, the main house—a symbol of fear—casts eerie red beams over this serenity and nearly destroys Porter's peace of mind forever.

IV.

LOST ECSTASY
(1927)

INTRODUCTION

Although mystery and suspense play a significant role in *Lost Ecstasy*, it is mainly a romantic novel with just enough intrigue for seasoning. In spite of lengthy description which tends to drag at times, a powerful theme weaves its way through to the end, and the effect is that Rinehart has in this novel cast a powerful spell.

With thrills of a different nature, this tale provides an exciting change from her cleverly written mysteries. At first Rinehart seems to be slightly out of her element when describing the West. But soon the narrative begins to flow and it becomes increasingly evident that she is equally familiar with the conditions of life in the western and eastern parts of the country. Rinehart was not writing this novel from imagination alone: her travels throughout the West and her interest in the plight of the Blackfeet Indians have been well documented.

In some ways, though, the mystery she introduces is disappointing. For example, Little Dog, the Indian, is strongly suspected of shooting Tom, a ranch hand, and this is, of course, an important element of the plot. We are left wondering about his guilt until the author rather abruptly states, "Little Dog had not yet come back to the Reservation, although shortly after he had shot Tom he left the show." The complexity of Rinehart's murder mysteries is absent here; in this story, mystery takes second place.

THE STORY

Kay Dowling was very young when Lucius died. As she studies a faded picture of him in his younger days, she notices a certain resemblance to herself. Years later, she happens upon that same photograph. It reminds her of the L. D. Ranch and she tells her father she would like to go there. Henry is not interested, but when he learns that things at the ranch are not going well, he cannot avoid making the trip. With old Lucius's private car attached to the end of the train, the entire family, along with Herbert, Henry's secretary, heads West.

As the four-day journey nears an end, Kay begins to feel a keen sense of anticipation and of coming home. Waiting on the car platform, she gets her first glimpse of Tom McNair and is deeply impressed. While Henry and Herbert worry about conditions at the ranch, Kay tries to fight her infatuation for Tom, but weakens when one morning he asks her to go horseback riding with him. Herbert mistakenly assumes that her relations with Tom are becoming serious and he decides to alert her father. In all fairness, it must be said that to warn Henry about this matter is against Herbert's code of ethics. However, with a little urging from Henry, he finally admits that Kay may be interested in Tom. Although Henry cannot believe that Kay is serious about a cowhand, nevertheless he is worried, and he decides it will be better if the family goes back East.

Meanwhile, Herbert tells Kay that Tom almost killed an Indian named Little Dog in a drunken brawl. Even though she knows the type of man Tom is, she finds herself making excuses for his bad habits. Finally, he admits his love for her, but insists that she forget him as he is not worthy of her love.

Tom leaves for the round-up full of anger and resentment that he has let himself get caught by a woman. Then early one morning the cattle begin to stampede. He knows the Indians are responsible when he finds the stripped carcass of a cow. Later, Tom is ambushed and during an exchange of gunfire he seriously wounds a brave named Weasel Tail.

Now returned to the East, Kay resumes her social life. Although her parents think she has forgotten Tom, she tells Bessie she has not given him up. Tom, on the advice of a stranger, decides to go East to get Kay. Unfortunately, the whole episode turns into a debacle and he returns without her. Shortly after Christmas, Weasel Tail dies. Tom goes on trial and is acquitted.

After his acquittal, he joins a traveling rodeo and wild west show. Everything is going well when Tom sees Little Dog, who has also joined the show, and he wonders if the tribe has sent the Indian to do him harm. However, for whatever reason Little Dog is there, he does not bother Tom.

In February, Kay agrees to marry Herbert. But one day as Kay is watching a parade, she notices an elegant-looking figure on horseback. It is Tom. Suddenly realizing what a long life lies ahead of her with Herbert, Kay decides to go to Tom if he wants her. In the morning, she finds him and they are married that same day. She tries not to think of what she has done, the unhappiness of those she has left behind, the scandal, and, of course, Herbert.

The show, now with Kay along, moves on to another town. Tom volunteers to help out an injured member of the troupe by driving a prairie schooner in a staged attack during which shots are fired. When this part of the performance is over and the firing stops, Tom is found lying on the ground, wounded badly in the leg. As a result, his ankle will always be stiff and he will never be the rider he was once. Who fired the shots is a mystery, as the Indians' guns had been loaded with blanks.

In mid-June, the Ursula newspaper announces that Tom Mc-Nair is home again, this time with a wife. As the couple settles into life in Ursula again, Tom comes and goes on mysterious errands and Kay assumes he is looking for work. Evidently she is the only person who does not know that he is convinced Little Dog shot him, and is determined to find him.

It is a difficult time for the two of them. Although Kay is trying to cope with her new life, the heat and loneliness are almost too much to bear. Tom cannot find work, but is too proud ever to accept any Dowling help. At times they quarrel but always make up. However, as she is left alone more and more, Kay begins to question Tom's absence. Little incidents occur that lead her to believe a girl may be the reason, and her thoughts run wild.

Then one day Tom sees Little Dog, almost chokes him to death, and lands in jail for ten days for the assault. Kay decides it is time to visit Mr. Tulloss at the bank to ask that he lend Tom some money to start a cattle business for himself. After a lengthy discussion, an agreement is struck, and Kay and Tom leave Ursula to begin a new life. Tom registers the L. D. brand as his own, and with the money loaned him by Mr. Tulloss, he buys horses and a work team.

Life is brighter for a while until the Indians, who still hold a grudge, threaten him again. Added to this, the country is so dry that there is little water available for the cattle. Discouraged, Tom tells Mr. Tulloss he will release him from their agreement, but the banker does not want him to give up.

His troubles are not over yet, however, as Clare Hamel is still trying to upset the marriage. Close to a nervous breakdown, Kay finally tells Tom she is going home, that her mother is ill, and she needs time to think things over. Feeling helpless and defeated, Tom assures Kay that he will never ask her to come back.

When Kay arrives home, the servants are the only ones who make her feel welcome. Although still upset with Kay, Henry agrees to let her stay on the condition that she not leave again until her mother, who is dying, no longer needs her. After three weeks, she writes Tom saying she will return to him as soon as she can, but that he must ask her first. He does not answer the letter. Still stunned by Kay's departure, he is trying to get on with his life. When she notifies him of her mother's death, she receives a short sympathy note, but no request that she rejoin him.

Tom has worked hard all winter and now has sixty-five calves with his brand. Filled with pride, he visits Mr. Tulloss to study their accounts. During their discussion, the banker advises Tom to go after Kay and bring her back. Happier than he has been in months, Tom heads back to his ranch to find that most of his herd has been stolen. The rustlers have ruined him.

Fully aware of the patience of Indians, especially Little Dog, he understands the ingeniousness of their work, how they waited all winter until the calves were fattened in the spring and summer before making their raid. Next he learns that Little Dog has been killed by another man. Since he has lost everything, even his opportunity for revenge, Tom leaves the ranch and returns to the traveling rodeo.

In the meantime, Kay has given up hope. Then, as before, the show comes to her city, and as she watches the parade, something strange happens to her. For the first time she looks back at the girl she was when she ran away with Tom and realizes her reason for marrying him was more of a romantic nature than true love. She saw him then as a carefree and reckless cowboy. But when Tom was having his problems, the excitement was gone for her and she abandoned him for the easy life.

The story has now reached its high point since, regardless of the outcome, Kay decides to return to Tom once again. And again he tries to discourage her. Realizing now that she must make the final move, and knowing that he has not changed and never will, Kay tells Tom she will not be sent away and will go wherever he goes. At long last, they understand each other probably as well as they ever will. Their faith is shaky, but their hopes are high and their love is strong.

SETTING

The setting is twofold: a large estate in the East, and the L. D. Ranch, a huge spread in the Northwest that supports thousands of cattle. When old Lucius Dowling died, he left the property to his son, Henry, and his daughter, Elizabeth Osborne. The ranch house, located at the base of the mountains, is made of field stone and furnished in the latest style. The view from the house is magnificent. Symbolic of life itself, the valley, treeless except where a stream flows from the mountains, spreads far and wide. Rolling grassy hills and dark yellowish-brown buttes resembling prehistoric monsters complete the panorama.

Some distance from the ranch is the busy town of Ursula, an attractive place with paved streets and even a railroad. In spite of all its activity, Ursula is no different from the smaller towns along the track.

Immediately beyond its fringes the back country begins, the summers are hot, dry, and dusty and the winters cold and windy.

All of this is in sharp contrast to the Dowling property in the East, where Lucius's son, Henry, and his family live. The huge estate is surrounded by trees and flowers. Inside, the house smells of "soap, furniture polish and fresh flowers." The family spend summers in the country, with a social life revolving around the Club.

CHARACTERS

Kay Dowling was the only person who cried when old Lucius's walnut bed, which had stood in one spot for twenty years, was moved after his death. Her grandfather had been an adventurous man and not above occasional easy sinning, but Kay grieved for his loss just the same. When she cuts her hair and takes up smoking, Henry, her father, thinks she is beginning to show signs of becoming like his sister, Elizabeth, known in the family as Bessie.

He is mistaken. Lucius left the ranch to his children, Henry and Bessie, "but those qualities of his which Henry had missed he had passed, without the sinning of course, to [Kay]." Lucius had been much disappointed in Henry, who did not share his zest for life. On the other hand, Lucius disapproved of Bessie because she was so much like himself.

A pompous man, Henry Dowling is too good, too proper, and too cautious. He is proud of his standing in the community and fond of his family, except for the troublesome Bessie. His wife, Katherine, is subject to weak spells and is already showing signs of failing health. Although Henry is good to her in his way, he is domineering and at times brutally harsh. She has forgotten the dreams of her youth; now she dreams of her daughter's future, hoping Kay's life will include love and marriage.

One of the most colorful but complicated characters is Tom McNair, top cowhand on the L.D. Ranch. Jake Mallory, the range foreman, tells Kay that Tom is "like a young colt, a bit wild and not halter broke yet." Stubborn, proud, and sensitive, he is confident around women and haughty about his ability to break, ride, and rope horses. Tom can be light-hearted and happy, but when Kay knows him better, she will learn that he can also be sullen and bitter.

Herbert Forrest, Henry Dowling's secretary, is a very methodical man. His daily routine follows a tight schedule and he is irritated if anything upsets this tidy ritual. With his trousers neatly pressed and his hair brushed just right, Herbert is a perfect picture of a gentleman. He has an annoying habit, however, of tapping a cigarette on the back of his hand. Herbert changes somewhat when he becomes engaged to Kay. He is self-assured and even jaunty to the extent that he takes to wearing a gardenia in his buttonhole. Although Kay knows he is "a man of her own breeding and stamp," she says later that "out West," such labels are reserved for a "pedigreed bull."

Among the important minor characters is Little Dog, who is mentioned often, but described only as a full-blooded Indian, heavy and muscular, with a wide face and tawny complexion. Nellie Mallory, one of Tom's many admirers, is jealous of Kay and so has very little to say to her. She is more passive in her behavior than Clare Hamel, who fancies herself in love with Tom and keeps busy setting traps and causing unpleasant situations for both Kay and Tom.

CONFLICTS

Conflicts add complexity to life and fiction alike. In *Lost Ecstasy*, characters encounter an array of conflict that pits them against nature, society, each other, and even themselves.

In earlier days, Kay never questioned the life she lived or her parents' right to control her every move. But when she meets Tom, she begins to wonder about the conditions she has always accepted. Even though Kay is now of age, Henry and Katherine unjustly continue to maintain certain powers over her, and she feels pressured by the certainty that there is no way out of the situation. Unhappily for Kay, but much to her father's relief, she agrees to marry Herbert. This, of course, is what those of her social standing expect of her. To marry a cowboy is unthinkable. She likes Herbert and knows she will be safe with him, but beyond that she cares little for him. And so turmoil rages within her.

Herbert's attitude toward Tom is one of contempt, while Tom is desperate, bitter, and resentful of Kay's family and their money. While Tom wins Kay, the victory brings him little peace of mind. He does love Kay, but he is also aware that he has scored a certain triumph over Herbert, the Dowlings, and the social milieu she has given up for him. His roots are deep in the soil, but he feels that Kay has "been superficially rooted in something quite different." He calls it society, but cannot define what he means in words. At any rate, he resents it even though he seems to have won over it.

Occasional quarrels between Kay and Tom point up their totally different outlook on life. When she asks him for a cigarette, he refuses. In fact, he forbids her to smoke. This is against Kay's way of thinking because she is of the "new school" which teaches that marriage is a mutual contract in which obedience no longer plays a part. The one thing they do share is their deep love for each other, but if that fails, they have nothing except their mutual poverty and mutual anxieties to take its place.

Few of the characters are without conflict in this story. Tom and the Indians, especially Little Dog, are constantly at odds with each other. The situation between Clare and Nellie is not a happy one, as they both want Tom's attention. Henry dislikes Mr. Tulloss, the banker from Ursula, because he cannot control him and because he helps Tom. Kay never cared for Uncle Ronald, Bessie's husband—and so the list grows until one wonders if Kay and Tom's love for each other can survive.

THEMES

This novel furnishes a keen insight into human relationships. One aspect of relationships is communication, a process problematic to many of Rinehart's characters here. For example, when Bessie asks Herbert about Kay's health and he dodges her questions, she says she has seen many lives ruined by people who remain silent when they should have spoken out. Kay does not hear from Tom in over three weeks and the strain on her begins to show. As she tries to assure herself that it is not over between the two of them, she thinks, "Two people who loved each other did not simply separate, without a word, without a farewell. Life might separate them, but not their own voluntary act."

Another thematic thread woven into the fabric of the novel involves pride. Katherine is more understanding of her daughter's feelings than Henry, who will never accept Tom, a cowboy, because of his lowly status. Katherine is concerned as to whether they are right in judging him as they do and wonders why they should assume that their way of life is best. Later, as though trying to appease "some old and possibly angry God," she visits the cemetery to place roses on old Lucius's grave.

It is not until Katherine is dying that Henry realizes over fifty years have passed and all he has to show for it are material things. He is losing his wife, he can no longer control his daughter, and soon he will be alone. Although his great wealth has provided temporary contentment, most of that joy and satisfaction has now evaporated. He has always had too much pride, which has been the cause of unhappiness for himself and others. When Henry has his weaker moments, the reader may wonder if he will relent. But this is not to be. Ultimately he remains the same old Henry: too proud, always suspicious, distrustful, and judgmental. Although Tom and Henry share some of the same characteristics, Tom's fierce pride hurts only himself and Kay.

Herbert also suffers from the effects of pride, but he differs from Tom and Henry in a way that surprises even himself. When Kay is about to leave him, he tells her, "'You can always come back to me...Good God, Kay,' he added. 'You have dragged me in the dirt, and still I can say that to you!...I have my pride...but I suppose there is such a thing as caring too much to remember pride.'"

Bessie, who has had an unsuccessful marriage, is plagued by the weight of experience. She offers Kay some advice regarding Tom, but realizes she has not helped. She feels "that she had been trying to teach a child higher mathematics. That was one of the tragedies of experience; it could never help any one else." The message echoes Rinehart's words in *The Circular Staircase*, when Rachel thinks, "But young people refuse to profit by the experience of their elders."

SYMBOLISM

In Rinehart's mysteries, the details of the various murders and character motivations tend to obscure many of the symbols. In *Lost Ecstasy*, however, they are easily recognized.

One scene depicts Nora, Kay's personal maid, as dismayed over Kay's broken mirror. The shattered glass distorts the reality of the visible world, and superstition holds that seven years' bad luck will result. At first thought, Kay thinks that seven years of misfortune is difficult to accept. Then suddenly she realizes that without Tom her "luck" is bad anyway.

Another symbol related to the visible world involves a memorable sunset. From her balcony at the eastern estate, Kay watches the sun setting in the West and in her mind's eye she sees the different colors of the mountains as the sun goes down behind them: first rose, a warm, active color; then blue, a cold, passive, retreating shade; and finally gray, representing inertia, gloom and depression—similar to the color of ashes. She sees in the sunset spectrum the pattern of her own life, first full of rosy promise and over time reduced to darkness, "like her life from now on."

There are other symbols, such as Kay's wedding gown. To her bridesmaids it represents more than just a gown: it means wealth and the joining of two people about whom they share "an eager half-neurotic curiosity." But Kay will never wear the beautiful gown. Instead, she leaves her heretofore ordered life—the conventional, signified by the gown—to marry Tom, her beloved cowboy. She rejects tradition to venture into an emotional and social wilderness.

Tom's horsemanship is a symbol that speaks strongly of his personality. He is literally on his high horse—a perfect picture of vanity—when he tightens the reins and lightly spurs the animal, which then rears in a gesture of defiance. When Tom loses his ability to ride and hence his mastery, it undermines his manhood and he becomes bitter, and poisoned by thoughts of revenge.

Tom's defiance must be broken, like a colt's, but so too must Kay's. Her rejection of Herbert for Tom is an overt act of defiance.

Not only is she trying to break away from the reins of her domineering father, but also from Herbert who, for her, represents the constraints and comforts of peace. Has she chosen wisely? From her world of good breeding she has become a newcomer in a "world infinitely remote."

V.

THE DOOR
(1930)

THE STORY

In *The Door*, Rinehart returns to the murder mystery genre. The narrator, Elizabeth Bell, a lady of high social standing, is unmarried and has lived alone for many years, with only servants for company. She has become so well acquainted with her house that she knows its moods, its good and bad days, and its peculiarities. And yet she realizes how little she knows about people—even those individuals closest to her.

The permanent staff consists of the butler, Joseph Holmes, a quiet, respectable-looking gentleman who has served Elizabeth for a long time; Robert White, her chauffeur; Norah Moriarity, the cook; and Clara Jenkins, the housemaid. Mary Martin, her live-in secretary, is young and efficient if a bit eccentric, and not one of Elizabeth's favorite people. Sarah, the middle-aged family nurse, has a room at the house, but also spends time with Laura, Elizabeth's sister in Kansas City, and with Katherine Somers, Elizabeth's cousin in New York.

The setting is in a section of the city that was once rural. Old-fashioned but comfortable, the house sits back some distance from the street, with stone gateposts at the entrance to a drive that circles around a grass plot before the front door. Behind the garage at the rear of the house lies a deep ravine. And, of course, thick shrubbery (familiar to Rinehart devotees) shields the house and is scattered over the grounds. On one side of Elizabeth's desolate property is an acre or two of undeveloped land called the Larimer lot, on which the first crime occurs. A light snow has fallen and the cedars at the top of the downhill path are especially beautiful.

Although Elizabeth lives alone, she is not lonesome: friends drop by, sometimes for bridge or a dinner party. Such a sedate household depends for its youth on visits from Judy (Katherine and Howard Somers's daughter) and Katherine's stepson, Wallie. With no idea of what lies ahead, Judy has arrived full of her usual enthusiasm, and

Wallie is coming later in the evening to inspect an old ormolu cabinet, which along with a sword-cane dating back to the Mexican War, spark the beginning of a carefully woven plan. A simple crime at the start, not meant to include killings, slowly escalates until four murders and three assaults have been committed.

Norah, the cook, finds the cane one day while housecleaning and Joseph, the butler, discovers a hidden blade in it as he is polishing the knob. This sword-stick once belonged to Elizabeth's grandfather, Captain Bell. She shows it to Jim Blake, her cousin, who is interested in owning the cane. Since Elizabeth does not like having deadly weapons around, she gives it to him, a gift that will, unfortunately, mean trouble for Jim.

The narrative opens with Elizabeth and Judy comfortably settled in the library and talking of family matters. The two dogs, Jock and Isabel, are asleep in front of the wood fire. Sarah, who has decided to go for her usual walk, appears in the hall and Judy suggests that she take the dogs with her. The nurse agrees. She never returns.

After Sarah leaves, Elizabeth and her niece continue their conversation. During a brief silence, Elizabeth happens to glance in the mirror over the fireplace and is shocked to see the reflection of a man crouched on the stairs. He seems to be listening; then, without a sound, he backs up the stairs. She rings for Joseph who, after a thorough search, finds no one. In the meantime, Judy summons a policeman but his search is also fruitless.

At one A.M., Elizabeth, who by now is very worried about Sarah, goes out to the street, instinctively moving toward the sound of barking dogs. Far back in the Larimer lot she comes upon Jock and Isabel tied to a tree, but Sarah is not with them. The next morning, Sarah's room is found in a shambles. Someone apparently had entered and examined family records now strewn on the bed. The police continue their investigation, convinced Sarah has simply disappeared on her own. A few days later, however, her body is found. She has sustained a blow on the head and two stab wounds in the chest.

This is only the beginning of the murderer's calculated moves. Dissension rules the house, fueled by fear and suspicion. Mary Martin accuses Jim Blake of receiving a letter from Sarah about the time of her death, but Jim denies this, even though Mary has proof that Sarah was writing to him. Now members of the family feel that Mary has become dangerous with her accusations and that Jim may be suppressing information.

Judy and her reporter friend, Dick Carter, are determined to solve the crime. One evening when Dick is out of the house, Mary goes alone to the garage tool room for a ladder. When she does not return, Elizabeth and Joseph go looking for her, and find her unconscious body lying on the tool room floor, struck down in the same manner as Sarah.

It was following Sarah's murder on April 18 that Judy was assaulted, but no further attempt was made on her life. Wallie, upset by the news, tells Elizabeth he will stop this thing if he has to kill someone with his own hands. But he refuses to explain. And still there are no clues.

Very little is known about the next victim, Florence Gunther, who rented a room at a Mrs. Bassett's boarding house nearby. It is possible Florence knew why Sarah was killed. Instead of going to the police she tried to see Elizabeth, and this was her undoing. On May 1, she is shot and killed. Her room has been searched and an attempt made to conceal the fact. Inspector Harrison is not sure the two women were killed by the same individual, but he thinks the motive for the first crime led to the other. Apparently certain papers or some physical property prompted the searches.

The sword-stick now begins to play a prominent part. Until Sarah's body was found, the sword-stick had been in the hall with Jim Blake's other sticks; then it disappeared. The timing of this disappearance leads Wallie to suspect Jim. When the district attorney questions Amos, Jim's servant, he learns that Jim had gone out one evening and had taken the sword-cane with him. Now Jim is under constant surveillance.

Meanwhile, still playing detective, Judy convinces Lily Sanderson, a boarder at Mrs. Bassett's, to let her and an unwilling Elizabeth into Florence Gunther's room to look around. In one of Florence's shoes, Judy finds a small piece of paper on which the following had been typed: "Clock dial. Five o'clock right. Seven o'clock left. Press on six." Judy takes it with her although it means nothing to either of them. Next, she and Dick dismantle all the clocks in the house in search of clues to correspond with the paper from Florence's room. They find nothing. Other puzzling developments continue when Wallie tells Elizabeth that she will know everything he does when the time comes.

The next victim is Howard Somers. Although he had had a bad heart, nevertheless his dying contributes to the mystery. As Dick Carter and Elizabeth learn more about the circumstances surrounding Howard's death, they wonder if another crime has been committed. Howard's attorney, Alex Davis, tells Elizabeth that Howard has left his money to the servants, certain charities, and Jim Blake. Also included is a trust fund for Wallie. But Wallie claims a second will in a New York bank revokes the first one. Alex says Sarah and Florence were witnesses to it.

Trouble piles upon trouble. Joseph is brutally attacked in broad daylight, but for what reason? Elizabeth begins to wonder if the murderer is one who kills for the enjoyment of it. What she does know for certain is that this person is wily and strong; he has no feeling for the lives of others; he resembles Jim in stature; her dogs know him; and his motive is carefully concealed.

Circumstantial evidence continues to build against Jim. When he is accused of visiting Howard Somers before he died, he denies it. Then the authorities surprise everyone by stating that Howard did not die of a heart attack, but of potassium cyanide poisoning. When Inspector Harrison discovers the missing sword-stick buried in the cellar of Jim's house, Jim is placed under arrest for the murder of Sarah Gittings, and is suspected in the murders of Florence and Howard. Although the inspector believes he now has the motive, he is not yet satisfied: he tells Elizabeth it appears that Jim is guilty, but some discrepancies still need explaining. Elizabeth and Jim think something happened in Howard's four-room suite at the Imperial Hotel to cause him to change his attitude toward his family and Wallie. What secret the rooms might hold is not apparent until Elizabeth's visit there.

After Howard's death, his wife Katherine moves into her brother Jim's house for a while. Since she neither likes nor trusts Amos, Jim's servant, she lets him go; in retaliation Amos gives damaging testimony before the Grand Jury and then disappears. He emerges from hiding long enough to tell Dick that he believes Jim is innocent. At this point, it is inevitable that something will happen to Amos, and it does. He is discovered drowned. At first the death seems accidental, but it is soon revealed that Amos must have been pushed into the water by someone who knew he could not swim.

Dick, searching for more evidence about the crimes, is the next victim. He is found unconscious in a gully, but lives to tell about it. Later, when Elizabeth is thinking about all that has occurred, she is amazed at how close they all had come to the solution without really seeing it. On several occasions, in spite of the unusual precautions taken by the criminal, he has barely missed being caught. Elizabeth's attitude toward the case is now colored by superstition. She believes the killer's identity will remain concealed by Fate until some unknowable mission has been carried out.

One day as Elizabeth is looking over Sarah's record of Howard's illness, she discovers two pages missing—August 12, the date on which the rough draft of the will was made, and the next page, dated August 13. This surprises her, but even more surprising is a note written by Sarah on August 11: "August 12th and 13th withdrawn for safekeeping. Clock dial. Five o'clock right. Seven o'clock left. Press on six." The Inspector thinks the clock dial may not refer to a clock, but to a hiding place. Evidently, the records had no value until Sarah learned the contents of the new will. Then, for some reason, they became important. Since Florence also knew about the new will, it now seems logical to assume that the missing two pages have been the object of the murderer's diligent search.

On June 9, Elizabeth's sister Laura arrives for Jim's trial. It finally gets underway on the following day and goes on for days. It seems to be a foregone conclusion that Jim will be found guilty. Then something in Judy's testimony causes Laura to inquire of Elizabeth if Sarah had told her about the cabinet. As Sarah had not, the two of them rush back to the house. Laura opens the center door of the cabinet and exposes twelve small bronze rosettes with one in the center, forming what might be considered a clock dial. When it is opened, they find it empty, but the lining is badly scratched. Someone has been there ahead of them.

On this same day, Wallie disappears. The evening before, he had called Judy to say he was going to testify and that he had a lot to say. He assured her that Jim Blake would not go to the chair. Wallie never shows up at the trial, however; Jim protests his innocence, but the jury finds him guilty of murder in the first degree.

The final attack is on Joseph, who is shot but not killed. Inspector Harrison asks Elizabeth how much she knows about Joseph's private life. He says the psychology of this crime differs from the others in that no effort was made to cover it up nor any care taken against being detected. The unraveling of the plot is now moving rapidly to its conclusion.

On July 17, Joseph is released from the hospital, but is still unable to do much work, so Elizabeth arranges to send him on vacation for a few weeks. He happily accepts her offer. On the same day Katherine, Howard's widow, decides to take charge and try to resolve matters. At her request, she and Elizabeth visit Mr. Waite, the district attorney, who also drew up Howard's new will. Katherine, believing the will is the key to the mystery, implies that the new edition is a forgery. She had been led to believe, through conversations with her husband, that most of Howard Somers's money would come to her when he died. Now Katherine has learned that in the new will Wallie is to receive half of the large estate. She neither understands nor accepts this. She also questions a $50,000 fund left to Wallie to be handled at his discretion. Alex Davis, Howard Somers's attorney, says he was told by Howard that Wallie would understand.

Waite agrees to accompany Elizabeth and Katherine to Howard's room at the hotel to re-enact his meeting with Howard on the day the new will was drawn up, and to prove to Katherine that he himself had not forged the document. Once in the bedroom, Waite is shocked to find that the door to the room is now on the other side of the bed, a fact that Inspector Harrison has known for about a week. Katherine, suddenly realizing that this may not be the same room Waite had been in previously, crosses the sitting room, looks into the other bedroom, and says, "I think this is where you came, Mr. Waite...to [Wallie's] bedroom, where an accomplice of [Wallie's] impersonated his father and drew that will."

This realization is the key that unlocks the entire case. We soon learn that the whole sequence of events was a conspiracy, including a plot that failed. If the plan had been successful, there would have been no killings. Fraud was the intent: murder was never contemplated. But one criminal act is like the first domino falling: it leads to another and yet another and unless it is stopped, results in total destruction.

The original plan was a simple one. Joseph blackmailed Howard Somers into paying $1,000 in return for keeping certain matters quiet, a claim that was not true. Later, when Howard suffered but survived a heart attack, his illness gave the greedy Joseph another idea, which he outlined to Wallie. Since Wallie needed money, he soon agreed to it. The plan called for Joseph to pose as Howard Somers; he would draw up a fake will and sign it in Somers's name. The $50,000 mentioned in the will as a special dispensation to Wallie was to be his share for the imposture.

Jim Blake is freed; Wallie, whom Joseph had almost killed, is found alive by Inspector Harrison; and Dick asks Judy to marry him. Harrison gives Elizabeth a detailed explanation of the case. Even though he is pleased with the manner in which he solved the mystery, he feels that he bungled the job in one important aspect: Joseph outwits the police by committing suicide with cyanide just as they are about to arrest him.

CONFLICTS

A mother asked her son one day how it would seem to have no disagreements in the family, to which he replied, "I should be uncomfortable because life is not like that." For some, discord is a way of life; others spend a lifetime fighting it. But where would a mystery be without opposing temperaments? There are many conflicts in *The Door*, a few examples of which can be presented as follows: Katherine Somers is jealous of Judy and Margaret, dislikes Wallie and Amos, and resents Joseph; Wallie Somers dislikes Katherine and Joseph, resents Katherine, and has a remote relationship with Sarah, Judy, Katherine, and Howard Somers; Jim Blake dislikes Wallie and has a remote relationship with Amos; Joseph and Sarah also dislike Wallie; and Elizabeth has a remote relationship with Howard Somers.

Judy and Dick's conflict differs from the others' because it involves love. Although Judy comes from a wealthy family, Dick feels, if they marry, that she should live on his salary. This problem is finally resolved, of course, because romantic troubles always have a way of working out in Rinehart's stories. Wallie's problems, on the other hand, are resolved far less felicitously. As the above discussion shows, he is disliked by practically everyone, and his position as an outcast may in fact be a strong motivation for the crimes he commits.

The discussion does not reveal anything unusual about Joseph: his craftiness is well concealed. He seems to be an excellent servant; only the results of his evil doings become evident. Whereas Wallie needs money, Joseph is greedy for it and will do anything to attain this end. Once Joseph takes the wrong road in life, his ambitions continue in an evil direction. Jealousy and lack of compassion also plague him, until finally he reaches the end of the road and runs out of control.

The problem of evil versus good is a difficult one to separate because it cannot be resolved in intellectual terms. Little light has been shed on the problem due to its many ramifications and the inability to understand it.

THEMES AND SYMBOLISM

Although similar in plot line, Rinehart's books often differ in respect to underlying themes and patterns of symbols. In *The Door*, thematic issues seem to take the forefront, while symbolism receives less emphasis. Determination in attaining an unselfish goal is commendable: greed combined with determination can lead in the wrong direction and prove deadly, as evidenced in *The Door*. These two themes afford Rinehart opportunity to study the human mind.

It is understandable that Rinehart may have been in a serious mood, with crime very much on her mind when she was writing this novel. After all, she herself had barely missed death at the hands of someone she'd trusted (see details in the following section). Thus the narrator here comes to see how betrayal can turn her trust to ashes, and how tangled are both events and human motives. In *The Door*, Elizabeth Bell learns that, just as the people around her are incredibly complex and unpredictable, most complex crimes are never solved by one method or one person without definite clues and distinct motives. In fact, all the murders in this mystery are finally solved by accident and by "the temporary physical disability of one individual" combined. None of these events evolve simply: appearances can hide untold tangles just beneath the surface.

Rinehart's study of the mind focuses upon Elizabeth, through whose eyes we see the events. That mind, we find, can be at times chaotic. Because Elizabeth kept no record of the crimes, she finds it difficult to tell about them in proper sequence. She has to contend with what her mind chooses to remember when painful memories instinctively try to slip away. Thus the author makes it clear that consciousness, like life itself, is far from orderly.

Sometimes when we do not understand a person's behavior, it is because the emotion he or she reveals is a mask that covers true feelings. This is the case with Wallie, a very nervous, sometimes belligerent, person. The anxiety he feels from his involvement in Joseph's plans takes the form of anger. Elizabeth later remembers an unpleasant interview with Wallie and realizes that she had no idea how terrified he was.

Once again Rinehart underlines the theme of appearances hiding a more complex reality. The idea of this unmasking of the true self extends even to Joseph. As evil as he was, who knows what was in his heart and mind when he devised the original foul plan, or when, in desperation, he swallowed the poison? What we do know, Rinehart seems to say, is that a dangerous mind will go to any length to achieve its purpose. Thoughts can be destructive, and like malignancies can in time devastate a human life.

The novel shares another element common to Rinehart's other books—romance. In this story, Dick and Judy are the symbols of normality in the midst of a very abnormal situation. Romantic interests serve to distract the reader from the riddles, easing the feelings of horror arising from the violence portrayed.

NARRATIVE SUSPENSE

In a number of Rinehart's books, *The Door* being a particularly good example, the author's writing goes beyond mere imagination and is based on actual facts. In 1927 Rinehart's cook, who had been with her for some twenty-five years, tried to kill the author. Fortunately, she was rescued by other servants in the house and the cook later committed suicide. The experience, she realized, offered possibilities for a story. She wrote the book for her sons, who had founded the publishing company, Farrar & Rinehart, and now needed a bestseller; it was a huge success.

One stimulating factor this mystery provides is grounded upon the beliefs of Elizabeth, the narrator of the story. The first two-and-a-half pages of the book deal almost entirely with her thoughts on crime, and additional observations are liberally scattered throughout the book. Through Elizabeth, Rinehart sets up a moral stance; this character sees the larger issues of life.

Chapter One begins with Elizabeth contemplating the past. It is clear that a character is speaking, but soon there is a subtle transition from her discourse on last night's roast beef to more philosophical matters. This kind of encounter with the more weighty questions of life lends a depth to Elizabeth's characterization, an authenticity that increases her credibility and strengthens her role as a sort of moral fulcrum upon which the events of the novel are balanced.

A final strong point in this novel is its factual accuracy. Rinehart's knowledge of police procedures is extensive and detailed. Her descriptions of effective methods of criminal follow-up lend credibility to the plot. It is apparent that the author has thoroughly investigated this phase of her work. Such authentic detail about police methods helps make the novels addictive.

VI.

THE GREAT MISTAKE
(1940)

THE STORY

Patricia Abbott leaves Miss Mattie's boarding house and drives up The Hill to The Cloisters to be interviewed for the position of social secretary to Maud Wainwright, but almost turns back. The huge buildings are a frightening sight to her, but once in the presence of Mrs. Wainwright, she relaxes.

The Cloisters, so-called because John C. Wainwright purchased an entire stone cloister from an old monastery, stands on what the people of Beverly refer to as The Hill. After Wainwright established his residence there, many others followed suit. The Hill, which was formerly used by those who live in the Valley for riding, hiking, and picnics, now has cement roads, a golf course, and a country club. Although there is no enmity between the two settlements, the people do not associate with each other. Now, Maud tells Pat she is planning to give a party to bring them together.

Pat agrees to help. She likes Maud, a big good-looking woman around fifty, with blond hair worn in a long braid. She tells Pat a little about herself, her beloved son Tony, and her deceased husband, John Wainwright. Because Pat will have to know her way around, Maud takes her on a tour of the place, which is indeed overwhelming. Pat learns later that Tony and his mother occupy only about six of the rooms, although there are twenty or more servants at The Cloisters.

The next three days are exhausting for Pat with so many dinner details to be taken care of. Thus, she is not in a good mood when she first meets Tony Wainwright, a young man she finds annoying and patronizing. In an effort to calm her, he shows her the playhouse, which has a pool, tennis court, living room, game room, kitchen, bedrooms, and baths. A delightful setting for the upcoming party, The Cloisters will become a place of horror.

Maud's dinner that night is a success. She accomplishes what she set out to do, to mend the rift between the village and The Hill.

During the party, Pat sees a man looking in the window. Apparently not a guest, he runs away when she approaches him. She says nothing to Maud about her experience.

One day, after Maud has left for the city, her friend Margery Stoddard comes to visit. Married to Julian Stoddard, Margery lives nearby at a place called The Farm. She asks Pat if Evans, the watchman, has seen anyone sneaking around. She had caught a glimpse of a man the night before and is concerned for her children. Meanwhile, a letter comes for Maud which Tony will not allow his mother to see. Maud returns from the city in a state of collapse, but she refuses to discuss what happened. The mystery has now begun.

Four days later, Maud is better but still acts differently. She requests that her attorney, Dwight Elliott, be summoned to make out a will for her. This surprises Elliott, because Maud already has a will.

The house is beginning to depress Pat, especially after Tony intercepts another message for Maud, a telegram, which he has no intention of delivering. Pat has good reason to feel uneasy when she notices that Roger the dog has been treading in blood. Roger leads her to the playhouse, where she finds an unconscious Evans. The watchman has been struck on the head and his trousers are missing. After the injured Evans is taken to the hospital, Pat contacts the chief of police, Jim Conway, who inquires if Evans carried anything important. Pat can think of only one thing: the keys to the house and all the buildings were attached to a chain on the pants. The next day, the trousers are found but the keys and also Evans's revolver are missing.

Near the end of August, although Maud has improved, she has lost her zest for life. Trouble piles on trouble: the house is broken into and a third message comes for Maud, the contents of which are shocking to Tony. He is not the only one who is disturbed: Dwight Elliott is concerned about Maud's collapse. From the nature of his questions and his apparent unhappiness, Pat feels there may be some friction between Maud and her attorney.

In September, Pat discovers the source of the letters and telegram formerly addressed to Maud. They were from Bessie, Tony's estranged wife, who now arrives, bringing plenty of trouble for everybody. When Maud reminds Bessie that she paid her $500,000 to leave and never return, Bessie nonchalantly replies that they can talk about it later. Maud is certain that she has a devastating plan in mind. When Elliott learns of Bessie's arrival, he advises Tony to divorce her because she will be in control of the Wainwright Company should anything happen to Tony and his mother.

Not long after, the house is again broken into, though nothing is taken. This is disturbing and puzzling, but the real trouble begins a few days later when Lydia Morgan, a longtime friend of Pat's, requests that she come to see her. She is upset that her husband, Don Morgan, who deserted her fifteen years ago, wants to return. Pat believes it is a trick. But Audrey, Lydia and Don's daughter, is pleased with the news, especially because this ends any thought of Lydia's marrying Bill Sterling, a doctor in town.

On September 12, Don Morgan arrives and gossip is rampant in the valley and on The Hill. He pretends to be ill, with the result that Audrey waits on him hand and foot. With Don home, Dr. Sterling stays away from the house.

The pace now quickens and the mystery deepens when Pat falls down an empty elevator shaft, landing on top of an intruder. The two of them collapse and Pat faints. By the time she revives, the person has gone. Could it be the same one who attacked Evans, and who has been in the house before? An uneasy Bessie asks Pat many questions about her accident. Later, Pat realizes Bessie is playing a game, which will continue for some time.

Although there is no indication of upcoming tragedy, a call from Lydia to Pat signals the first warning: she is worried about Don, who has not returned from a dinner at the country club. Sunday morning, his body is found in a ditch: he has been dead for several hours. An autopsy reveals a scar on Don's chest. Dr. Sterling and the coroner agree that it is not a shrapnel wound as Don had always claimed, but a tattoo, possibly that of a girl's name beginning with a "J."

Jim Conway realizes that Don Morgan's death is a relief to many people, Bill Sterling among them. When questioned, Dr. Sterling says he did not kill Don. He may have had a motive, however, because of his dislike for Morgan and his love for Lydia. He tells Conway, "Find out why he came back and you'll know something." At this point Jim asks Bessie if she ever knew Morgan. "No...how could I?" Bessie indignantly replies. That evening, however, she tells Pat she once met a man in Paris by that name, but doubts that he was the same one. Pat does not believe her. Later, when Pat and Lydia are searching Don's room for clues to his murder, in one of his suits Pat finds a series of numbers on the label which she recognizes as the license numbers of Maud's limousine.

One week after Don's murder, Evans disappears from the Beverly hospital. For some reason, the news disturbs Bessie and she wants to leave town, but Hopper of the homicide squad prevents her from doing so. She is angry and afraid of something. Because she spends a great deal of time in her room with the door locked, Pat believes that whatever Bessie fears may be in the house.

Then, on October 8, when Evans's gun is found in Bill Sterling's desk drawer, Bill is arrested. The police are certain that he is their man, and the evidence seems to point in that direction. Later, Pat begins playing detective, and questions Lydia about a gun Lydia found in Don's room. At the time, nobody had been shot, but fearful of firearms she hid the gun in a hatbox and forgot about it. Then, when the Evans story surfaced, Lydia wondered if the gun belonged to him.

The more she thought about it, the more worried she became that Don might have been the one who attacked Evans. With this in mind, she buried the gun in the garden. Audrey saw her, dug up the revolver and put it in Bill's desk drawer.

Both Lydia and Audrey are questioned by the district attorney but are not held. Lydia's honesty works in her favor, and it is determined that Audrey's only motive for putting the gun in Bill Sterling's desk was simply that she thought it was Bill's. Although the district attorney's office still suspects Sterling, not enough evidence is available to hold him any longer. He is released the next day, but kept under surveillance.

Things quiet down for a while until one evening Bessie does not return from a trip to the city. Pat and Gus, Maud's chauffeur, decide to check on her. They find Bessie unconscious behind the wheel of her car, which has crashed into a tree. Revived, she claims that somebody shot at her. Tony is suspected.

The characters who know something of the inside story can offer several explanations. The general public, however, is concerned that a lunatic may be on a rampage. Maud is in a state of bewilderment and Bessie is terrified. She sincerely believes that Tony tried to kill her, but refuses to talk unless, as she says, "I have to."

One day, Maud shows Pat the contents of her wall safe. Although her health is better and she may live a long time, she wants to make some arrangements "just in case." Maud is concerned about a large brown envelope which she asks Pat to give to Tony if anything happens to her. She says he will understand.

Following another period of peace, the real tragedy occurs. After one of Bessie's parties, Roger the dog is heard whimpering by the door; the chain is missing and it is unlocked. Roger leads Pat to the playhouse where a fire is burning in the fireplace. Although everything seems to be in order, it is clear that someone has been in the living room. When Pat leaves the house, she walks toward the swimming pool and that is when she finds Maud lying beside the pool—dead. Although nobody knows how Maud died, Dwight Elliott offers the opinion that she committed suicide. He asks Pat to open Maud's safe to see if her jewels are still there. They find the safe unlocked, but nothing has been taken except two seemingly unimportant items: the list of jewels and the envelope for Tony. Neither Tony nor Jim Conway believes that Maud killed herself. Jim thinks she went to the playhouse that night to meet someone. He adds, "First we have to find out why Don Morgan was killed. That's the key to the whole thing."

Then Jim has an idea. He is curious about the contents of the missing envelope. Thinking Maud may have burned it, he suggests to Pat that they check the playhouse fireplace. Sifting through the ashes, he finds nothing, but Pat discovers the list of Maud's jewelry wedged against the chair cushion. Jim concludes, "She came down here to sell that stuff or to discuss selling it; and for some reason she was killed."

After Maud's funeral, the house is again broken into and her room searched. Bessie has left The Cloisters, and now that Maud is gone, Pat realizes she cannot stay there any longer. But first, she has an important matter to clear up with Margery Stoddard, and the two agree to meet by the Stoddards' pool. Margery tells Pat that fifteen years ago when Don left Lydia, he ran away with a Marguerite Weston (now Margery Stoddard). They married and after he left her, she divorced him. This occurred in Paris. Financially depressed, she was working as a stenographer with the American Express Company when Julian Stoddard walked in one day and recognized her as having once worked in his office in Beverly. After hearing her story, he paid for her return trip to New York. They became better acquainted and later married. Happy in their new life on The Hill, she and Julian were frantic when they learned that Don was back.

Then one night, Bessie informed Margery that she had known Don in Paris and he had told her everything. Margery, not wanting her identity nor any of the details known, was forced to pay Bessie for her silence. When Don's body was found, Margery thought Julian might have murdered him. Julian, however, not aware that Margery was being blackmailed, was unmindful of any threat to expose their story. Therefore, he had no reason to kill Don.

The meeting over, Margery leaves and it is then that Pat hears someone near her. This is all she remembers for two days. During this time, Julian Stoddard is arrested. Because Pat was struck down beside Stoddard's pool, the police believe it was Julian who tried to kill her and that he may have murdered Morgan. By the time Pat is well enough to sit up, Julian's case has gone before the grand jury and he is indicted.

The puzzle is far from solved. Pat herself is beginning to wonder if there is a madman around. Unusual happenings began when Don Morgan returned after fifteen years: Evans disappeared; Bessie arrived at The Cloisters and then left suddenly; and Maud Wainwright was killed. The household staff are convinced that Bessie is the villain. In spite of all the trouble, Tony, who has risen considerably in Pat's estimation, takes time out to tell Pat how much he loves her and that he hopes they can be married some day. Pat is willing. Once more Tony seems at peace, but not for long: Bessie is back.

Jim Conway, who has been striving to find the answer to the murders, is finally "on the track of something." He finds an article in the newspaper which, although not helpful in identifying the murderer, gives some inkling of a strange tale. He has a talk with Bessie, who becomes hysterical when he questions her about Maud's death and what she had expected from the Wainwright will. He thinks she knows much more than she is telling. Hopper, the district attorney, plans to call her as a witness to prove his case against Julian Stoddard, but Bessie never takes the stand.

Shortly thereafter, Pat moves back to Miss Mattie's. Even if Pat had wanted to stay at The Cloisters, Bessie makes sure it would be impossible when she says to her, "If Tony wants an affair let him have one...I'm not a jealous woman. But it won't go on under this roof." Then she adds, "I'm not divorcing Tony, and he's not divorcing me." Although Pat is now living at her former boardinghouse and working during the day at The Cloisters, she never sees Tony or Bessie there. Dwight Elliott, however, comes in to go over Maud's papers and her private files. In the meantime, Maud's room is locked because Bessie has been trying to gain access to search through Maud's possessions.

A touch of sadness is added to all the trouble when Roger the dog is poisoned. Whether or not it was deliberate is not known. It is a precursor to another tragedy about to strike The Cloisters when Bessie makes the same mistake Maud did: she decides to tell everything she knows. The next day she is found murdered, never having the chance to reveal her secret.

Once again, Dwight Elliott pays a visit to Pat. For some reason he looks tired and worried. Just before leaving, he asks Pat to "regard [their] conversation as strictly private." Just then, the telephone rings; it is Margery Stoddard and she wants to see her. Pat is surprised to learn that Evans is Margery's stepfather. After she eloped with Don, Evans was so angry that he threatened to kill him if he saw him again. Thus, when Don was murdered, Julian was certain of Evans's guilt. Margery is also concerned that her stepfather may be responsible for Bessie's death because he knew that Bessie was blackmailing her. The situation looks bleak for Evans and Julian.

Pat thinks the best thing to do is to tell Jim Conway the whole story. Meanwhile, Jim has set a trap for the murderer, who then commits suicide in an elevator at The Cloisters. The murderer meets a grisly end and the plot unfolds. We find that Maud's first husband was Don Morgan. Her full name was Jessica Maud, which accounts for the "J" tattooed on Don's chest. Tony, their son, remembers nothing about him except that he had been killed in the war. Five years later, Jessica Maud married John C. Wainwright. Believing that Don was dead, Maud made the great mistake of marrying old J. C. two years too soon for her marriage to be considered legal. According to the law, she should have waited seven years. Maud did not know that Don had divorced her and was still alive. She saw him that day she went to the city, which was the reason for her collapse.

Some time after Don left Maud, he married Lydia. He and Lydia had a daughter, Audrey, who had been dating Don and Maud's son, Tony. Then Don deserted Lydia and ran away with Margery, whom he also left. She later divorced him. Bessie, Tony's wife, was intimate with Morgan in France, probably saw the scar on his chest, and knew about his marriage to Margery. Such complications presented themselves to Bessie as an opportunity to extort money from Maud and Margery.

Donald Morgan was not fundamentally a bad sort, except for his love of women. At the time he was involved with Bessie, he did not know she was his son's wife. Further, he evidently meant no harm to Maud. He had tried to notify her that they were divorced, but the messages never reached her because Tony intercepted them. Since he could not get through to Maud on the telephone, he broke into The Cloisters several times, to no avail. Maud was not aware that the Don Morgan who had married and then deserted her was the same man who was murdered. A day or so after his death, she saw his picture in the newspaper and was so shocked she suffered a heart attack and nearly died.

Because Maud still did not know of the divorce, she felt she had done Don's daughter Audrey a disservice by not telling Lydia the whole story. She may have felt that she could make restitution to Audrey by selling her jewels and giving her the money. Wife or no wife to J. C. Wainwright, Maud had been given the jewels by J. C. If, as she believed, she had no legal right to the Wainwright money, she could nonetheless do as she liked with the jewels. Therefore, she probably had plans to meet with Lydia at the playhouse that night to confess everything. But her plans were never carried out. Someone made sure of that by killing her before she had a chance.

This is the story Pat recorded and relates to us. Tony has helped with a few details, and has himself learned some things. When Tony asks about Evans's death, Pat says she believes his asphyxiation by a gas stove was accidental. Julian is released from jail and the killer is exposed as Maud's attorney, Dwight Elliott.

Pat suggests that Elliott probably never meant to murder anyone. But even a man of good character sometimes falls victim to a fatal flaw that destroys what is otherwise admirable. "From nothing, he had built himself a strong position in the Wainwright Company. Not only wealth, but prestige." Then when Maud told Elliott the whole story about her illegal marriage to J. C. Wainwright, he was probably desperate. She said she had decided to turn everything over to the Wainwright family and leave. As the family's counsel, Elliott earned $50,000 a year and had hopes of marrying Maud to assure himself of a steady position. The pattern Dwight Elliott fell into is a common one: jealousy, which leads to anger, then hatred, and finally murder.

CONFLICTS

Bessie is a sparkplug of conflict in this novel. She stands out as the one who is disliked and resented more than any other person. She is, after all, perceived to be selfish, ruthless, and fundamentally lacking in integrity, and as such she further strains relations that are already under pressure. Her suspicious behavior makes it logical to pinpoint her as a likely suspect. But we find in the end that she is not a murderer—a troublemaker, yes, who changes the lives of many people and later becomes a victim herself.

Oftentimes, discord among the characters has little bearing on the plot. This is an effective device for the author to employ in order to obscure the facts and increase the level of complexity of the mystery.

THEMES

It is not enough to say that murder is the central idea in *The Great Mistake*. As the reader will discover, Rinehart has spun a web so complicated that when untangled, it reveals other relevant themes. For example, confusion abounds as to who was, or still is, married to whom, not to mention illicit affairs and quasi-incestuous liaisons. Out of this, a dark side of life evolves, a suggestion of the corruption arising from affairs among certain family members.

Another theme concerns human weakness. For women like Bessie, men and money are terrible temptations. Although from a respectable family, she is a clever but ruthless woman who works her way into society with no feeling for those she victimizes. Bessie never learns that responsibility goes with wealth and possessions.

Don, on the other hand, causes many of the problems in the novel through his insistent philandering and consistent unfaithfulness. His weakness for women speaks of a certain moral malaise that spreads like a net over others in the book, entrapping them in its fateful strands.

Another common Rinehart theme involves a clash between social strata, here embodied in the characters of Pat and Tony. Pat, who comes from a poor family, does not attempt, nor even imagine herself, to be in the same class with Tony. She wins his love, however, through honest and unintentional ways. Along the way, her judgment of him changes. She learns that a manner she may have perceived as patronizing might really have been self-assured. Her views of a higher social class must be modified somewhat for her to accept Tony and the world he represents.

NARRATIVE SUSPENSE

Dwight Elliott, who moves in and out of the story, is probably the one to whom the reader pays the least attention. Out of forty chapters, he is mentioned in only half of them. References to him are often casual and do not seem important at the time. Although subtle and well-spaced, clues to the murderer's identity slowly build like a mist rising from the sea. Problems are so numerous in this story that the reader may get lost in the mist and therefore not notice some of the obvious clues. A definite pattern emerges, however, which in retrospect is recognizable.

His visits to Maud are frequent; he asks Pat to talk with her about her lavish spending; he tries to convince Tony to divorce Bessie because he is worried about Bessie's controlling the Wainwright Company should Tony or Maud pass away; he is attentive to Maud at a tea she gives for some old friends; he asks Pat about her conversation with Maud the night before her murder and wonders if it was confidential; he thinks he should examine the safe; he makes arrangements for Maud's funeral; in her will, he is left $20,000, a small sum compared to the $50,000 a year he earns as counsel for the Wainwright Company; he tells the police something which sends them in search of Bessie; he has a long talk with Pat and requests that she regard it as private. All these suggest that Elliott is a decent counsel trying to do the best for his client.

When the reader finally learns that Elliott has been the culprit all along, the mist surrounding his true nature still does not lift completely. Near the end of the novel we are told, "That was when Dwight Elliott shot himself." An explanation follows, but somehow the ending is anticlimactic. After three hundred pages of clues and motives, the solution seems vaguely unsatisfying.

VII.

THE HAUNTED LADY
(1942)

THE STORY

Hilda Adams, whom Inspector Fuller affectionately dubs "Miss Pinkerton" because of her shrewd mind and quick eye, has been given an assignment at the Henry Fairbanks place. It seems that Mrs. Fairbanks has been catching bats in towels. Also, every now and then a rat plus a sparrow or two have joined in the fun, even though it is questionable how any such creatures can get into her room. At any rate, nobody believes her.

"Miss Pinkerton," alias Hilda, has just finished with one case and is reluctant to take on another so soon. She finally agrees to look into the activities at the Fairbanks house, however, and after depositing Dicky the canary in its cage at her landlady's door, she walks to the taxi stand and asks the cab driver, Jim Smith, to take her to Ten Grove Avenue.

Jim, aware that Ten Grove Avenue is the Fairbanks' address, tells Hilda of "talk" going around that "the old lady...thinks she's haunted," but not to let it bother her. Although Hilda assures him she is not easily frightened, she feels a bit lonely when he leaves. Suddenly she remembers walking by this very place twenty years ago when she was a student at the hospital; the house was bright and alive on the day that Eliza Fairbanks's daughter Marian married Frank Garrison. What seemed to be so beautiful then had ended in divorce. Even though the neighborhood is different now, the large red brick house with its iron fence still remains as a symbol of defiance against any outside changes.

The interior, which probably used to be glamorous and bright, is now quiet and gloomy, though not rundown. The long main hall is "well carpeted, the dark paneling waxed, the furniture old-fashioned but handsome." Across from the library, what were once two parlors are now joined together into a Victorian-style drawing room whose "yellow brocaded furniture" and "crystal chandeliers" are quaint, if not outmoded. The huge kitchen, a cheerless room in need of painting, has a coal-fired range "long enough to feed a hotel." Close by is an old-fashioned pantry with worn linoleum on the floor and shelves full of dinnerware.

On the second floor, the room that Hilda will use faces a side street where from the window can be seen a stable with a cupola. Street lamps and a gleam of light from the corner market brighten the edges of the estate. Janice Garrison, Eliza Fairbanks's nineteen year old grand-daughter, has the room behind Hilda's. Mrs. Fairbanks's son Carlton, a former broker, and his wife, Susie, have the two chambers across the narrow hall from Hilda and Jan. In the front of the house where the hall widens, a large landing is used as a sitting room, and the two front corner bedrooms belong to Jan's mother, Marian, and Eliza Fairbanks herself. On the third floor, rooms formerly used for guests now have cloth-draped furnishings and show no signs of activity except for an occasional cleaning.

It is important to describe Eliza Fairbanks's room in detail since this is where much of the action in the novel takes place. Large and square, it has four windows screened and barred, two facing the front and two on the side. Her four-poster bed stands along the wall opposite the side windows, and on the other wall is a fireplace set off by closets that smell from old and unused articles of clothing. Except for a radio, the room seems to have changed little since Eliza first moved in. A heavy bureau, a rocking chair, and a faded picture of her husband, Henry, all date back many years. The only contemporary item seems to be a small safe built inside one of the closets. Later, after thoroughly inspecting this room, Hilda will agree that it is "as tight as a drum."

Hilda Adams, who is thirty-eight but looks younger, has been a trained nurse for fifteen years. She is a quiet person and a good listener, so people tend to open up to her. As she listens to them, she "sits and knits" and talks about her canary, and soon they are confiding everything to her. She is useful to someone who needs a trained nurse, and even more useful to Inspector Fuller, who says Hilda "can see more with those blue eyes of hers than most of us could with a microscope." By the end of the ensuing two weeks, the Fairbanks household will see her more as a sharp-witted detective than a nurse.

Hilda watches Jim's taxi disappear down the drive, then rings the doorbell. Janice answers the door. Before taking Hilda to Eliza Fairbanks's room, Jan gives her some background information, emphasizing that her grandmother has a sound mind even though it may not be apparent from her odd behavior. While talking with Hilda, Jan hears a door open across the hall. Her father, Frank Garrison, who shows his forty-two years but is still a handsome man, has been visiting there with his second wife, Eileen, Jan's former governess. At thirty-five she is quite pretty but sullen looking. Janice introduces them to Hilda, explaining later that her father can come to the house only when Marian is not at home.

When at last they reach Eliza's room, which she keeps locked, Janice taps on the door. Eliza slowly turns the key and warily peaks out. Remembering Eliza Fairbanks as having been a stately woman, Hilda is startled to find her "incredibly shrunken." Dressed in a quilted house coat, she looks old and frightened. When Hilda was a girl, Eliza Fairbanks was recognized in social circles as Lady Fairbanks. As a former board member at the hospital where Hilda worked, Lady Fairbanks's visits there "had been known to send the nurses into acute attacks of jitters." Now she has become bitter and suspicious, though not childish. When dressed in black silk and sitting in her rocking chair, she is still domineering and her small eyes are bright, shrewd, and somehow pathetic.

Eliza tells Hilda she does not want to be nursed, only watched over, as someone is trying to frighten her. She issues strict orders not to disturb her, but to maintain a vigil in the hall just outside her door. So for the entire time Hilda is on this case, she is to spend every night keeping her eyes open, using her bedroom for sleeping only in the daytime, as it is not the days but the nights that worry the old lady.

Now that Hilda has arrived to serve as sentinel, Eliza wastes no time in displaying her first piece of evidence to prove she is not crazy. She has captured a bat in a towel. She says that in the last month or two she has seen three bats, two sparrows, and a rat in her room. This sudden onslaught of wildlife has convinced Eliza she needs help; so she wants Hilda to find out how and why the animals are getting in. Eliza shocks Hilda with one more piece of information: three months ago she had almost died from arsenic sprinkled on her breakfast strawberries. Jan had called in Dr. Courtney Brooke, who lives on Huston Street across from the Fairbanks stable, and since the day he saved Eliza's life, he has been her personal physician.

When questioned about possible suspects, Eliza tells Hilda she suspects everybody, but trusts the servants more than her family. The one person she did trust, Frank Garrison, was lost to her when her daughter Marian divorced him.

It is not surprising, therefore, that Eliza has given no one the combination to the safe. She says she never opens it because there is nothing in it, but Hilda cannot believe this, as the old lady wears a sly expression when she makes that claim. Up to this point the reader may wonder if Eliza is being manipulative, since she harbors resentment toward certain family members and may be pitting them against each other.

The first evening on the case, Hilda has just settled into her chair in the hall when the radio in Eliza's room blares forth and continues until after midnight, then stops abruptly. Next Hilda is startled by a pathetic figure coming up the stairs. It is Marian Garrison, who was once a beautiful woman, but now at thirty-eight presents a tragic picture. Dressed in black, she is very thin and haggard-looking. After Marian goes to her room the house is quiet, but Hilda thinks Eliza is still up and about. She hears what sounds like the creaking of a closet door and the radio starts to play again.

Suddenly from the bedroom a shriek louder than the radio is heard. Eliza finally unlocks her door and, sure enough, there is a rat under the bureau. Miss Pinkerton's work has now begun in earnest. She notices that Eliza's clothes are placed neatly on a chair, the windows are closed, and the bed is hardly mussed. By the fireplace, a card table is set up with a pack of cards on it. Eliza says she was playing solitaire.

The next day, Hilda makes a survey of the servants. There are only three in the house now: William, Maggie, and Ida. William, who is old and given to few words, has been there for thirty years; plump, middle-aged Maggie the cook, for twenty years; and Ida, a pale, listless woman, is relatively new, having arrived ten years ago. The only other servant, mischievous, ill-natured Amos, lives over the stable. After listening to their conversations, Hilda decides that they are loyal, uneasy, badly frightened, and innocent.

Most of us, unless we have the entire picture of a situation, can jump to wrong conclusions. Since Hilda has been at the Fairbanks house only a short time, she cannot know why the family troubles run so deep. What Hilda lacks in information she makes up for in good sense and insight; having appraised the household staff, she seeks further information from Dr. Brooke. He tells her the Fairbankses are "a decent lot...but there isn't anything to hold them together. They fight like cats and dogs." He's right about that. At a very unpleasant noon meal with the family, Hilda notices the differences among them, the intense dislikes and resentments. Thinking about this later, however, she cannot believe that murder was in the air.

One day, during the time Eliza is out for a drive with her daughter Marian, Jan brings Eileen to the house. Upon learning of this, Marian is furious and later becomes hysterical when told Eileen is expecting a child. That evening, without any notice, Marian packs up and leaves. Ida, who helps with the baggage, is the only one to see her go. A few nights later, Eliza Fairbanks is murdered as she lies sleeping, stabbed by an unknown assailant. It is late Saturday night when Eileen once again comes to the house. She says Frank has left her and she has no other place to go. She is put in Marian's now vacant room for the night. Sometime after midnight, Hilda is startled by stealthy footsteps on the third floor. From the foot of the stairs, she can see a figure moving quickly and noiselessly. When she reaches the top, there is no one there. Later, she realizes that the three minutes she was away from her post was time enough for someone to stab Eliza. The only other time she left her place outside the door was when she went to the kitchen for fifteen or twenty minutes, but Dr. Brooke had agreed to stand guard. When asked if he had remained in the hall, Dr. Brooke admits to having visited Janice for five minutes or so.

For some time now things have been happening that Hilda has seen but has not understood. So she decides to take some action. A series of events reinforce her move in this direction. Standing by her open window, she sees Jan leave the house and apparently enter the stable. She follows her and after some confusion finds her unconscious on the floor of the loft. After examining Jan, Dr. Brooke says she fell and then was struck with a flashlight. Whoever did it could have killed her, but for some unknown reason, did not.

Hilda is doing rather well with her detective work, but infuriates Inspector Fuller when she fails to notify him immediately about Jan. Still, he cannot help admiring her. After all, he did assign her to this case.

The next puzzling event occurs when Ida disappears. She is later found at the morgue. An autopsy reveals she was poisoned.

What more can happen? Just two things—and then "Miss Pinkerton" can rest her case and return home to her canary, her books, and her soft bed. First of all, Marian attempts suicide but is saved by Dr. Brooke and Hilda. And just as everyone is recovering from this scare, the final curtain falls: Eileen kills herself with Frank's revolver.

CONFLICTS AND MOTIVATION

Everyone in the family has a motive for killing Eliza, which is not surprising because their conflicts and motivations are closely intertwined. However, the various loves, hates, and petty jealousies among the family members hardly seem reason enough to kill the family matriarch. It is true Eliza was a domineering woman, but for the most part she kept to herself and furthermore did provide a home for them. For a number of reasons, though, living there only intensified their feelings of resentment toward her and toward each other. With the tension mounting, something dreadful was bound to happen to one of them, but why was Eliza Fairbanks the victim? What could be gained from her death? Robbery seems unlikely since she had always maintained there was no money in her safe. The motive must have been something else.

Marian is a logical suspect as she has lived (unwillingly) at Ten Grove Avenue since she was married and blames her mother for the failure of her marriage. She is also bitterly jealous and resentful of Eileen, her "replacement" in Frank's affections. Eileen is disliked by the Fairbanks family, but Marian's daughter Janice continues to be friendly toward her. Carlton and Janice are probably the only two who have any love for the old lady. Jan has stayed on because she feels that her mother and grandmother need her. Carlton, who has nowhere to go, is of course discontented, and Eliza and Susie, Carlton's wife, do not get along. He and Susie want to buy a farm, but since his business failed they have had to accept Eliza Fairbank's charity.

Everybody knows something about the family tensions, but each one is either quiet or evasive about his or her respective piece of the puzzle. Susie finally admits she was afraid of one thing: she had found out that Eliza had been selling off her securities and keeping the cash in the house. This, she felt, could be dangerous for everyone if it should become common knowledge. "Suppose she had two or three million dollars in cash in this house?" Susie says. "A lot of people might know...it wasn't safe. *We* weren't safe."

With the entire family pulling in so many directions against such suffocating boundaries, it is no wonder that one of them was driven to the madness of murder.

THEMES

All that has happened almost assuredly points to the work of one person—Eileen. It is Hilda's belief that this strange and unpredictable woman is not quite normal. When and why her aberrant behavior originated, however, is not known. But being married for seven years to a man who still loves his first wife angered her and may have helped push her over the edge. Anger, hatred, fear, and the ever-present desire for money are very strong emotions. Separately, it may be possible to cope with any one of these feelings, but together, such components often become a time bomb. Who knows what lights the fuse? Eileen may have been somewhat unstable, but for other reasons the evidence against her is sufficient to show that she was capable of murder. She had admitted hating Marian because she knew that Frank still loved her.

As Jan's former governess, Eileen had been more of a mother to her than Marian, whose attention had been directed toward an active social life. Did Eileen pull the ladder out from under Janice, causing her to fall? The reader is not certain of this, but she could have killed the girl had she wanted to, as Eileen was, we find, the one who struck her with the flashlight. At the time, she may have had one of her lucid moments, or then again, her affection for Janice might have overpowered her killer instinct.

When Eileen's attempt to poison Eliza failed, she tried a new strategy. Perhaps hoping to frighten Eliza out of the house or to scare her to death, Eileen blackmailed Ida into putting the various creatures through a hole in the wall. This plan worked fine until she suddenly realized that Ida knew too much and was filled with terror. So as a reward for her help, Ida received five hundred dollars and a cup of poisoned tea.

Thus far there are three emotions dominating Eileen's actions: hatred, fear, and anger. These emotions add up to an even stronger one: revenge! It was not so much for money but for revenge that Eileen killed Eliza. Apparently, Eileen knew about an agreement written by the old lady whereby Marian's alimony would cease when her mother died. Carlton observes when he reads the document, "So that's why she was killed." The reader is not told how Eileen learned of this, but it is suggested she taunted Frank until he revealed the information. Eliza's insistence on witnesses to the agreement indirectly contributed to her murder, since when more than one person is involved, a secret loses its definition.

Now for the inevitable happy ending à la Hollywood: in spite of all the troubles in her stories, Rinehart always finds room for romance and humor. Jan and Dr. Brooke are going to be married; Carlton and Susie are planning a second honeymoon; Marian and Frank Garrison will probably remarry; and Dicky the canary is asleep in his cage—Hilda Adams is back home again. Even Inspector Fuller asks "Miss Pinkerton" if she would object to his dropping by now and then. Thus, the tensions within the family have been reduced so dramatically that these characters, formerly so caught up in bitterness and resentment, can go on to happier lives.

VIII.

THE YELLOW ROOM
(1945)

THE STORY

It is Thursday, the fifteenth of June. Carol Spencer and her mother are aboard a train to Newport, Rhode Island, where Mrs. Spencer will stay for a week or two with her married daughter, Elinor Hilliard. The following Sunday, Carol will continue on to Maine to open Crestview, the summer house at Bayside. She is uneasy about going, but Mrs. Spencer insists that it is just the place for her son, Gregory, to spend his thirty-day furlough from the war in the South Pacific, and that his fiancée Virginia can visit him there.

On Sunday, Carol takes the train to Boston, where she meets Freda, Maggie, and Nora, the three servants who will accompany her to Crestview. Carol assures them that Lucy Norton, wife of the caretaker, will have the house warm and breakfast waiting. But when they arrive, no one greets them. The house looks unoccupied and inside, the air is frigid. Even more unpleasant is a strange odor that smells like the remains of a fire.

Moving throughout the house, Carol finds evidence of someone having been there, especially in the library, where she notices an ash tray containing a partially smoked cigarette with lipstick on it. A sense of panic overtakes the four of them; Freda wants to leave immediately, but Maggie, the Spencer's cook for twenty years, tries to settle them down. Her efforts are futile: there are no groceries in the supply closet; even the coffee can is empty. She suggests to Carol that Lucy, who usually orders the groceries, must have somebody sick at home. Freda returns from the cellar where Maggie sent her for coal and Maggie gets ready to light a fire. The strange odor is not too powerful in the kitchen, but as soon as Maggie pours kerosene onto the coals and sets a match to it, Carol senses a similarity to the smell they encountered when they first came in.

Certain that something has happened to Lucy, Carol tells Maggie she is going into the village to check on her. Her concern is only part of her reason for leaving; her unease has grown so intense that she feels she must get out of the house for a while. Shivering from the cold, Carol heads toward the village a mile away. She considers stopping at Colonel Richardson's, but as yet does not feel like seeing him because he will want to talk about his son, Don, to whom Carol was once engaged. Don is believed to have been a war casualty, but the Colonel will not accept the fact.

Carol finally arrives at Harry Miller's market and walks in. When she asks Harry if he knows anything about Lucy Norton he is evasive, but then says that Lucy fell down the staircase at Crestview and broke her leg. She is recovering at the hospital. Harry further reveals that one cold night when she went to the linen closet for a blanket, somebody reached out and knocked the candle she was holding out of her hand. The intruder then pushed her down and ran off. It was then that Lucy, getting up in the dark, fell down the stairs. She was found later by old William, a helper at Crestview. One last bit of information Harry offers is that he noticed a light in an upper corner room on that same night. From his description, Carol recognizes it as the yellow room.

Back at the house again, Carol is telling Maggie the news when suddenly Freda lets out a scream from upstairs. Staggering down the steps, she enters the kitchen and falls in a dead faint. Carol tells Nora to get a blanket from the linen closet to cover her. Soon after Freda revives, a pale Nora returns and says in a calm voice, "There's somebody dead in the linen closet... There's been a fire there too." Carol checks the closet herself. The servants were right: there is a body of a woman.

Once again, she trudges down the hill to the village, this time to tell Floyd, the chief of police, what has happened. Floyd drives Carol back to Crestview and on the way, he notices Major Jerry Dane slowly limping up the hill. They stop. Floyd introduces him to Carol, explaining that Jerry was wounded in the war and is on leave to recuperate. He suggests to Dane that he might like to help investigate a death at the big house. Jerry is skeptical, but interested. Upon arrival, the two men go upstairs to view the body. Soon after, Jim Mason, Floyd's assistant, and Dr. Harrison, who is also the coroner, join them. After examining the body, Dr. Harrison determines that the cause of death is a "bad frontal fracture," and agrees with Major Dane that the woman was dead before the fire. They also believe she is not a local resident.

Carol knows she has to call Elinor at Newport and ask her to tell her mother the news. And she must also visit Lucy at the hospital. On her way to the garage, she meets Freda, who says that the yellow room has been occupied recently. A thorough check of the area confirms Freda's suspicions, but something is wrong; no clothing is around and the closets are empty.

Somewhat later when Carol returns to the first floor, she is surprised to hear a male voice in the hall. A man by the name of Starr from the press has heard about the murder and wants to talk with her. Having seen the body earlier, Starr describes it from his notes: "age approximately twenty to twenty-five... Bleached blonde. Possibly married... Silver fox jacket, no maker's name. Clothing under body not burned..." Carol says she does not know who it is.

News travels fast. Soon neighbors and acquaintances visit Carol to sympathize "and—if possible—to get a glimpse of the closet." The elderly Wards, who live on the property adjacent to the Spencers' place, are among the visitors. For some reason, each time the corpse is mentioned, the Wards look uncomfortable. One by one the people leave, until only Marcia Dalton, a nurse's aide at the hospital, remains. When Marcia mentions Elinor, it is evident she has more on her mind than small talk. Finally, Marcia says she thinks she saw Elinor's car speeding toward the railroad station about two o'clock Saturday morning. Carol tells her she must be mistaken because Elinor has been in New York.

That night, Carol calls Elinor to tell her what Marcia has said. After a pause, Elinor says that she has an alibi. She gives Carol an account of her whereabouts on Friday and Saturday and then hangs up abruptly. Two questions remain: why did the girl come to Crestview, and if Lucy knew about it, why did she let her stay? Just then, Jerry Dane arrives. Feeling she must talk to someone, Carol blurts out the whole story.

In the meantime, Floyd arrives, bearing some burned articles of clothing. While he is questioning Carol, Jerry finds a pine needle in one of the scorched bedroom slippers. Although Floyd maintains that the murder occurred in the house, Jerry notes that the girl may have gone outdoors. If so, "It might change things somewhat." The next morning, Carol has a call from her mother, who is more upset by the notoriety and disgrace of a killing in her house than by the murder itself. She orders Carol to return immediately, but Carol says she must stay for the inquest because the authorities believe the family may be involved.

Some justification for her statement is borne out by the doorman at the Spencers' apartment house on Park Avenue. The morning Carol and Mrs. Spencer left their residence, a young woman resembling a stranger later seen at Bayside had asked for Miss Carol Spencer. Carol does not hear about this until some time later. In the meantime, she is upset that the police are not allowing anyone to see Lucy Norton until the inquest.

That same day, Colonel Richardson, who says he has just learned about the murder, comes to offer his sympathy. When Carol tells him nobody knows who the girl is, he replies that certainly Lucy Norton must know. After the colonel has left, Jerry arrives. He asks

Carol to help him search for the dead woman's burned clothing which he believes may have been buried on the hill. Their search is fruitless, but a shovel covered with clay and dried leaves that Jerry finds in the tool house may be helpful. He takes the shovel with him and Carol returns to the house.

She goes upstairs by elevator in which she finds a bobby pin with a blond hair in it. Carol is not yet aware that her discovery is of any consequence. In her room, she tries to straighten out the mystery by asking herself questions, but cannot come up with any answers. Finally, she calls Elinor and tells her she needs help and wants her to come to Maine. Elinor gives several reasons why she cannot come, but agrees when Carol reminds her about Marcia seeing her car. Meanwhile, Jerry, who has been combing the hillside again, discovers a large metal piece in the form of the letter "M," possibly from a woman's purse. He is now more certain than ever that the girl was killed outside and brought into the house.

Elinor arrives on Thursday, the day of the inquest. Sullen and complaining, she asks Carol if she will have to testify. Carol says it is advisable if she knows anything. Later, in Elinor's room, as Carol is helping with the unpacking, she is shocked to see several pale bobby pins, the same color as Elinor's hair, on the dressing table. Hoping that she will trust her enough to tell the truth, Carol describes her elevator episode. However, Elinor, genuinely surprised, assures Carol she has not used the elevator in a long time. At the inquest, the coroner tells the group the body has not been identified, but "there [are] indications that she had borne a child." As more witnesses come forward, Elinor tries to leave, but Carol stops her. Jerry, who has been observing Elinor, is convinced she knows something.

When Lucy Norton is brought into the room in a wheelchair, Jerry notices that her arrival is a shock to Elinor. Lucy says the girl had come to the house and had asked for Carol who, she said, was expecting her. Lucy let her use the yellow room to freshen up and then agreed to her staying overnight. The name she gave was Marguerite Barbour. During the night, Lucy got up to get an extra blanket from the linen closet, and this is when it all happened.

That evening, Carol and Elinor accept a dinner invitation at the Wards' home. Carol notices that neither one looks well. In fact, Mrs. Ward is especially nervous. She tells Carol that Floyd, the chief of police, was asking about Gregory and she thinks Greg should not come to Crestview. After dinner, Mr. Ward accompanies the women up the hill to their house and Carol wonders at his apparent relief as he leaves them. At one A.M., Carol is awakened by the fire siren; the entire hillside is ablaze. It takes about two hours for the firemen to control the fire. When they are gone and the house has quieted down, who should walk in but Captain Gregory Spencer, tall, blond, and dressed in his uniform. He asks how the fire started. Then, realizing the lateness of the hour, he suggests they talk about it tomorrow.

Just before daylight, Carol glances out the window. Across the patio she sees Elinor's door open and close and realizes she has gone to talk with Greg. But she is too tired to give it any thought. The next day, Greg finds Jerry Dane inspecting the hillside; he introduces himself, and Jerry develops an immediate liking for Greg. He tells Greg that he thinks the fire was set in an effort to burn the dead girl's clothes, which he believes may be somewhere on the hillside. Meanwhile, Floyd's watchman on the hill has found another metal initial; this time, it is a "B." An old pitcher which had contained gasoline is found in the shrubbery, and Floyd is sure the fire was set with gasoline.

Jerry decides to talk further with Marcia Dalton, who is certain she saw Elinor's car that night. She tells him that Mrs. Ward also saw it; she had gone to look for her husband who sometimes goes for a walk at night, but was gone longer than usual. It was then she saw the car with a male passenger speeding down the hill from Crestview, but did not see who was driving. Next Jerry questions Nathaniel Ward about the matter. Ward protests that his wife cannot be sure of what she saw because of her poor eyesight and the darkness of the night. After Jerry leaves, Nathaniel goes upstairs and scolds his wife for talking too much. Then he tells her he must go out. On the way, he stops in his dressing room, picks up his gun, and puts it in his pocket.

Some time during that evening, tragedy befalls Lucy Norton. A nurse finds her the next morning on the floor near her bed. The doctor believes she died from shock and fright. Meanwhile, Carol is beginning to suspect Elinor of being involved in the mystery, and she decides to check Elinor's room. In her closet is a woolen housecoat which Carol has never seen. Upon inspection, she finds dust and sand-burrs stuck to the hem. Other than that, there is nothing to indicate that Elinor had worn the garment outside.

While Carol is puzzling over her findings, Jerry is steadfastly working on the case in his own way. He visits Lucy's husband, Joe Norton, and concludes that Joe knows nothing except what Lucy had told him. Later, Jerry goes out to take his turn watching the Spencer house. It is raining, and somewhere close by he thinks he hears a car backfire, though he cannot be sure because of the thunder and heavy rain. As he approaches the house and walks quietly around it, he discovers the front door ajar. He goes in and knocks on Carol's door and is relieved to find her there. She tells him she had locked the outside door before going to bed. He suggests that they check to see if anyone has left the house. Greg is sleeping, but Elinor has gone out. Outside, Jerry flashes his light up the hill and discovers Elinor, who has been shot but is still alive.

When the ambulance arrives, Carol accompanies Elinor to the hospital. Greg is in such a state of shock that Jerry offers to do the driving. At the hospital, Greg tries to comfort Carol as they wait to hear about Elinor's condition. At the same time, Jerry is becoming restless. After waiting for some time, he decides to leave, and makes his way to the Spencer residence. It is now after three in the morning. In spite of the late hour, the lights are still on in the house, but the front door is locked and no one appears to be there. Jerry goes around to the kitchen where, through the window he sees the servants gathered around and obviously frightened. He taps on the window. When Maggie recognizes Jerry she lets him in. He says he would like to check Elinor Hilliard's room for any possible clue to her going out.

Because Jerry finds no clues in Elinor's room, he goes into the yellow room where he is amazed to find complete disarray. One thing he notices especially is a piece of baseboard pulled out of the wall. Evidently this had been a good hiding place for something. He also checks Greg's room, although everything seems to be in order there. The next morning, Jerry examines the hillside again. As he is walking gingerly through the remains of the fire, he comes upon a small hole and a trowel lying nearby. Then he notices a footprint. As Jerry is comparing it with his own. he hears a movement behind him and looking up, sees Nathaniel Ward standing there. Nathaniel assures Jerry that the footprint is not his. When asked if he heard a shot the night before, Ward says no, that he has just learned about the assault on Elinor from the milkman. After the conversation has ended, Jerry continues on his way. Suspicious of Ward, he looks back and sees him pick up a shiny object which Jerry feels sure must be the shell from the gun.

Following breakfast that morning, Jerry visits Carol, who has returned from the hospital. After some discussion concerning Elinor's apparently stable condition, he is ready to leave when he meets Colonel Richardson, who arrives completely upset that nobody has told him about Elinor. Jerry has the feeling the Colonel is not telling all he knows.

On the hill not far from Crestview are two or three vacant summer houses. It suddenly occurs to Jerry that any one of them might be a good spot for someone to hide, and he decides to take a look. The first two show no signs of occupancy, but the third has a shutter loose and beneath the window are footprints. After some effort, Jerry manages to open the window and climb inside, where he stumbles over some blankets on the floor. In a kitchen cabinet, he notices some dishes that are unusually clean for having been stored several years. In one of the bedrooms, a pillow on the bed is slightly hollowed out as though someone had slept there recently. Except for the blankets, whoever had been using the house was careful to cover up any obvious evidence of his or her presence. Jerry leaves the same way he entered and drives home.

The last thing Maggie wants is to cause Carol more worry, but she has something important to tell her. Coming home from a late party the night Elinor was shot, Maggie heard the same noise that Jerry had described. Frightened, she waited a few minutes, and then she saw somebody running down the lane: it was Colonel Richardson. She thinks it strange that he should be out in the rain at one o'clock in the morning, dressed in what looked like a bathrobe.

Meanwhile, Jerry, whose mind never stops working on the human equation he is attempting to solve, pays a visit to Floyd. He asks if the dead girl was wearing a wedding ring when she was found. Floyd shows him a narrow gold band with the initials "C to M" on it. Jerry takes the ring to a watchmaker to be examined, returns it to Floyd, then drives to Crestview to see Greg. Convinced he has solved one unknown factor, Jerry asks Greg "just when and where [he] married the girl who was killed in this house ten days ago." He asks Jerry how he knows about the marriage. When Jerry mentions the ring, Greg responds that he never gave her one. Nonetheless, Jerry had learned from the watchmaker that Floyd had mistaken the "G" for a "C" in the ring's engraving. He confronts Greg with this evidence.

Greg decides to tell Jerry his story. Briefly, it seems that he was in Los Angeles a year ago on a special assignment. Having completed his work, and with nothing to do while waiting for a plane back, Greg joined a group of men who picked up some girls. A drinking bout followed, and a day or so later, he awoke in a room in Mexico with a girl whom, she said, he had married. Greg remembers nothing of a wedding.

The experience disturbed him deeply. He returned to the Pacific war zone where he tried desperately to get killed, but instead was awarded a decoration for bravery. For a year, he continues, he tried to end his engagement to Virginia, but could not bring himself to tell her what had occurred. Therefore, when he came back to the States on leave, he was in a dilemma because Virginia had gone ahead with their wedding plans. Greg tells Jerry he did not kill Marguerite Barbour, although he knew she was coming east. He sent her a thousand dollars to keep quiet, hoping all along that she would divorce him, but she would not.

Greg asks Jerry what he knows about the rest of the situation. In short, Jerry says that Elinor is involved and is withholding information. Greg tells Jerry they must get her to talk because it seems likely that Greg could be accused of murder. However, because Elinor has developed a fever, she is not allowed to see anyone and so any help she might offer will have to wait.

Jerry decides he needs a respite from the mystery. He invites Carol to go for a walk, which provides an excellent opportunity to tell her he is in love with her. He feels, however, that he has no right to expect her to marry him, partly due to her memories of Don and also to the uncertainty of his returning from the war. In a subtle way, Carol does not discourage Jerry when she says, "Would that matter so much? If the woman cared..."

Realizing that he can do no more until Elinor is better, Jerry goes to Washington for a few days on personal business. Upon his return, he learns that Floyd has arrested Greg for murder. The next morning, Floyd shows Jerry the murder victim's clothes, which have been found in a shallow hole on the hillside. Jerry tells Carol and then gives her Greg's entire story. Carol understands now why the police arrested her brother, though she is convinced he is not guilty.

Since Greg's arrest, Floyd has eased security at the hospital, thus making it possible for Jerry to visit Elinor. She is reluctant to talk with Jerry but when he mentions her brother, she says angrily, "These fools!... Arresting Greg! He never killed that girl." Even so, Jerry says that Greg may have to stand trial because several people are withholding information. When he tells her the story as he knows it, evidently he is close to the truth, as she objects very little except to say she did not kill Marguerite. She does admit setting fire to the hillside. Only partly satisfied with what Elinor has told him, Jerry is leaving the hospital when he meets Dr. Harrison. It seems the doctor needs a nurse for Mrs. Ward, who has had a stroke. Jerry suggests Marcia Dalton, not realizing until later that his idea is a brilliant one.

Marcia, having agreed to stay with Mrs. Ward for one night, wonders why Jerry has warned her to be careful and to keep her eyes open. The house is quiet when she arrives at nine o'clock and everything seems normal. At midnight, the doorbell rings. Marcia steps into the hall in time to see Nathaniel Ward going down the stairs with a gun in his hand. But it is only Colonel Richardson, who says he just heard about Mrs. Ward. The next morning the telephone rings. Marcia answers it. A man calling from San Francisco asks her to tell Ward not to worry, that everything is all right. There is no other message.

Greg has been in jail a short time, while Jerry is working hard to prove his innocence. One day, Jerry takes Carol to Pine Hill, where earlier he had checked out the vacant house. He asks her if she would like to look for further evidence of someone living there. Eager to help her brother Greg, Carol wastes no time and soon she discovers some cans of food hidden under a box. Dane warns her not to tell anyone what they have found because "it might be dangerous."

After driving Carol back to Crestview, he stops to see Floyd and finds Colonel Richardson at the office. The Colonel says he wants to share some information which he hopes will keep Greg Spencer from being indicted. He claims he saw, but did not recognize, the man who shot Elinor Hilliard. After a rather lengthy explanation, he concludes that he suspects Terry Ward, the Ward's grandson, because the man he saw that rainy night ran toward the Ward house, and because he was not as tall as Greg. He believes, however, that the shooting was accidental.

Jerry would like to talk with Ward, but feels this is not the time for it. Instead, he decides to see Elinor again. When asked if she plans to let Greg be convicted for a murder she knows he did not commit, she looks horrified. Finally, she answers, "I can't say I was here that night. It would wreck my life..." Because Elinor won't talk, Jerry knows he must find the solution somewhere else. He tells Carol he is flying to the West Coast, where he hopes to get more information.

The hearing begins a few days after Jerry leaves. Witnesses come and go, many questions are asked and details surrounding the murder are told. At last, Greg's attorneys do the unusual: they request that Greg be allowed to speak for himself, and permission is granted. But his testimony does not help. The next day he is indicted for murder in the first degree.

On Monday night, Jerry returns to New England. An uneasy feeling prompts him to take a walk to Crestview, where he finds Tim Murphy looking up the road. Tim is a private detective from New York and a friend of Jerry's who has been acting as gardener, but who really is there to protect Carol. He tells Jerry he saw somebody going up the hill and wonders if anyone lives up there. As Jerry heads for the vacant house, he notices a light moving up and down and around as though someone might be looking for something. As he gets closer, suddenly a branch catches his sleeve and snaps loudly as it breaks. A shot rings out; he is hit and falls unconscious.

Later, at the hospital, Tim explains the circumstances to Carol. He heard the shot and was on his way up the hill to check on Jerry when Floyd and his assistant, Jim Mason, drove up with the siren screaming. Someone had telephoned Floyd that there was a death at Pine Hill. But fortunately, the bullet had only grazed Dane's head. The next day, Jerry has an unexpected visitor. Starr the reporter sneaks up the fire escape to tell him he knows the person who reported Jerry's shooting to the police. Jerry thanks him, but says he also knows who it is.

Early the next morning, Nathaniel Ward stops by to see Jerry and tells him all he knows about the tragic happenings. "I'm glad to talk," he says, "it helps a little. I've carried a burden for a long time, and a sense of guilt, too."

The pieces of this intricate puzzle at last fall into place. Elinor arrived at Crestview shortly after the Colonel struck Marguerite, who was probably trying to extort money from him. Elinor found the dead woman but, knowing the victim was Greg's wife, remained silent to protect her brother and herself. Nathaniel Ward came upon Elinor leaning over the body. He carried the victim up in the elevator to hide the body in the linen closet and buried her clothes on the hill. Fearing involvement in the murder, Mrs. Ward set fire to the linen closet in hopes of destroying evidence of Marguerite's identity. The pattern of deception repeated itself when Elinor set fire to the hill, hoping to burn the clothes and, more important, the birth certificate she had seen in Marguerite's purse. Lucy Horton knew of the murder, but out of loyalty to the family told only part of the story to the grand jury. When Don paid Lucy a visit to persuade her to keep silent, she had a heart attack and died. The shootings were both accidental; Don was trying to scare Elinor and Ward was trying to run Jerry Dane off from Don's hiding place. The Colonel, already distressed by the news that the woman he struck was dead, discovered that his long-lost son was in fact alive. The good news was too much for him and he collapsed and died.

CONFLICTS

It is a literary commonplace that conflict is the heartbeat of a story. If so, then life is one huge heartbeat. But conflict is not all bad: if everyone agreed, many problems would never be solved. The manner in which antagonism is handled determines the outcome. In *The Yellow Room*, many outcomes are unpleasant because the characters choose to solve their problems in ill-advised ways. Thus, unhappiness, frustration, and disaster make up the heartbeat of this story.

Carol's reasons for unhappiness are numerous: since her father's death she has had the responsibility for the care of her mother, who is a fretful semi-invalid; she shares an uneasy truce with her sister Elinor; her hopes of marrying Don Richardson are dashed by the war; and her mother insists on reopening the house at Bayside, a house she has never wanted to see again. Thus, her family responsibilities prevent her from joining the Wacs or Waves or being a nurse's aide, and she is deeply resentful. She also resents Major Jerry Dane's attitude toward her. Realizing that Dane does not approve of "what he called people like her," Carol wishes she could tell him how useless she feels. Then she thinks resentfully, "Why should she? Just because he had been wounded in Italy did not give him the right to criticize those who could not fight."

It seems to Carol that Colonel Richardson, Don's father, harbors a grudge against Jerry Dane and she is right. As Carol and Dane begin to show an interest in each other, it is obvious that the Colonel is disapproving. Because he still thinks his son is alive, he wonders why Carol, who does not share his belief, will not wait for Don. "In a way it was like a silent battle between them, one of strategy rather than the firing line."

By the same token, Don had always resented Greg for reasons Carol cannot understand. Perhaps, she thinks, he was jealous of Greg, who is good looking, owns a plane, and has money. That jealousy may have led Don to make Greg the fall guy in the marriage to Marguerite. At any rate, the conflict between the two is underscored by the fact that one is arrested for a crime he did not commit.

THEMES

Although the interaction of characters plays a special part in this novel, it is important mostly for the effect it has on Carol's future. The net of deceit is woven from strands of loyalty and good intentions, for the people around Carol are trying to protect one another just as surely as Jerry Dane takes it upon himself to protect her. Carol's life can never be the same. The revelations of that summer certainly must weaken her faith in her siblings and indelibly color her dealings with them from that point on. By the same token, however, Carol has found a new person to trust; Jerry Dane and her impending marriage to him signifies a positive step for her in many ways.

One of the most important steps involves Carol's ties to her mother, and this in itself is another Rinehart theme: the parent who continues to dominate her children long after they have reached adulthood. Elinor is fairly well out of reach of her mother now, as is her brother Greg, but Carol, finding herself "in the position of the unmarried daughter," feels trapped, useless, and uneasy. The mystery, Carol's contributions to its solution, and the relationship with Jerry that grows as a result of the events at Crestview all contribute to a growing sense of worth and independence in Carol. She becomes a woman in her own right, not just an extension of her mother.

As in *The Swimming Pool*, class conflict is a strong thematic concern. Social status is of the utmost importance to Elinor, who is "capable of going to almost any length to avoid scandal and to save her social position." Included among these are aiding and abetting a crime and perjuring herself. Vanity motivates much of Elinor's behavior, and Rinehart uses Elinor to personify the selfishness and lack of integrity of the idle rich. The author quite pointedly draws a sharp contrast between Carol and her sister.

Another theme concerns Nathaniel Ward and Colonel Richardson. As Jerry Dane thinks to himself, "The picture of the two elderly men, each suspecting the other, was rather pathetic. It was the old story...no one being entirely frank. It was the same with every crime." Selfish motives undermine trust, the foundation of human relationships, so that even these two old friends find themselves at odds.

NARRATIVE SUSPENSE

Although the plots of Rinehart mysteries may follow similar patterns, the books often contain factual information and human insights that add to their realism and depth. In *The Yellow Room*, for example, Jerry Dane is a man who muses upon the nature of things. When revealing clues to his peers, "Dane, watching all the faces, realized that the difference between surprise and fear was very small. They all looked shocked. In a way, they all looked guilty." This character is three dimensional, fully human.

In another passage, Jerry "thought over the widening circle of every crime, the emotions involved, the people who were hurt, the lives that were blasted. War was different. You killed or were killed, but you left behind you only clean grief, without shame." Jerry is not just a tool to be used in the solution of the mystery; he is a thinking, feeling character who catches and holds the reader's attention.

SYMBOLISM

Although symbolism is sometimes difficult to understand, its purpose is not to hide but to reveal, using a simple mode of communication that involves representation. Jerry Dane adopts the symbol X from algebra as he attempts to solve a complex equation involving people instead of numbers. He finds that the equation has pluses and minuses. For Colonel Richardson, for example, his son Don is a living force, while to Carol he represents only a memory. This symbolizes belief in two ways: X positive and X negative. And yet, perhaps the symbols should be reversed. The Colonel is obsessed with the idea that his son was not killed in the war, which in many ways is a negative quantity, whereas Carol has accepted the fact that she has lost her fiancé, perhaps a more realistic, positive quantity. Carol signifies this quantity by removing Don's ring, a symbol of love and commitment, from her finger. This upsets the Colonel; he believes Carol's act stands for faithlessness and disloyalty.

Crestview itself is another powerful symbol. Since Lucy Norton's accident and the discovery of a body in the linen closet, the huge Spencer house has taken on a different meaning for Jerry. Up to now, "the place had been merely an ostentatious survival of an era that was finished," a time when the house was a locus of life and vitality. Now it is a place of death, symbolizing a biological facet of nature. How quickly an object emblematic of longstanding beauty can change when the surrounding circumstances do.

IX.

A LIGHT IN THE WINDOW
(1948)

CHARACTERS

Elizabeth Wayne, a small, resolute woman in her fifties, is still slim and attractive. Her smooth face is marred only by her mouth, which has a hard, determined look about it. One of her main concerns in life is that her son grow up in a good neighborhood. Her hopes and plans are not only for her son, but for herself as well.

Matthew Wayne, husband of Elizabeth, is a publisher with definite ideas on the types of books he accepts for publication. He is a good man and strongly family oriented. Although he seldom goes to church, he is profoundly religious.

Courtney Wayne, only child of Matthew and Elizabeth, is twenty-six years old. At age twenty-four he felt he was a man, and like many at that age, he was impulsive and sure of himself. Added to this need to assert himself, "he was lonely and bored in an army camp" and soon to be shipped out; it is not surprising that he fell in love and married quickly.

Frederica (Ricky) Wayne, the central character and lovely twenty-year-old wife of Courtney Wayne, comes from a small town in Ohio. Although a generation apart, she and Courtney's father share old-fashioned ideas and are compatible in this respect. She is, however, uncomfortable in the rich surroundings of the Wayne house and fearful of Elizabeth, her mother-in-law.

Jeffrey Wayne, son of Ricky and Courtney, is an important character because his actions will later parallel those of his father in wartime and in the publishing business.

Emmy Baldwin, a friend of Courtney in his younger and wilder days, spends a great deal of time trying to break up his marriage to Ricky. Emmy finally fades away, thanks to Roberta Truesdale, Matthew's sister, and Adele, Courtney's secretary, who are successful in defeating her efforts.

Dave Stafford, Ricky's brother, a happy-go-lucky young man, introduced her to Courtney. His mother described him as "high-strung." Because he was killed early in the war, the reader becomes acquainted with him mostly through the eyes of those who knew him.

Mrs. Stafford, mother of Ricky and Dave, has been a bitter woman since her son died. Usually stern in appearance, she relaxed whenever Dave was around. Of the two, he was her favorite.

THE STORY

In November 1919, Elizabeth Wayne is expecting her son Courtney home from the postwar Army of Occupation, but the war has ruined her plans for him. Two years earlier, he had married in haste, which essentially ended her ambitions. Now she resents his wife Ricky.

For the two years Court was away, Ricky stayed with her own mother. Now, however, she is living with Matthew and Elizabeth Wayne on New York's Fifth Avenue near Central Park. It has been so long since she has seen her husband that she is apprehensive about his impending return. She wants some time alone with him to get acquainted, a request that infuriates Mrs. Wayne.

Something as yet undisclosed happened to Court when he was in Germany with the occupation troops. For some time now, Ricky has not had any letters from him, and she is concerned. Added to her woes is the news that her brother, Dave, has been killed in the war.

At last, Courtney's transport ship comes in to the harbor in Virginia. Although he is happy to be coming home, he feels uncertain about what lies ahead. As hard as he tries to forget Germany, he finds himself thinking about the German family with whom he lived for a while. Readers are told that Court fell in love with Elsa, one of the daughters of Professor Hans von Wagner and his wife, but knows he must erase the memory of her. As the ship crowded with men moves closer to the dock, Courtney is excited to see his family waiting there. He greets his parents easily, but has forgotten what Ricky looks like; to him she is a stranger.

Their reunion is a rocky one. Courtney tries to talk to Ricky that evening, at the Shoreham Hotel, but she feels she is with a stranger. She confesses she has been concerned that there is someone else. Words follow which offer no satisfaction to either one, until finally Courtney leaves to spend the night in another hotel. Matthew, Elizabeth, and Ricky return to New York; a week later, Courtney arrives. Slowly and with uncertainty, he goes up to his old room, where Ricky is staying. He is pleased that the expected confrontation does not occur.

Later, Courtney's thoughts again turn to his new life. His father wants him to join his publishing business, but he is uninterested at

first. Eventually, Matthew tells him his business is failing, and Courtney takes the challenge and offers to invest his own money.

When Roberta, Matthew's sister in London, and her daughter,
Sheila, move in, Elizabeth objects, but is forced to give in to her husband. Roberta likes Ricky. Realizing that the girl is unhappy and
knowing the reason for it, Roberta suggests that she move away. Never
one to take a stand, Ricky at first rejects the suggestion, but Roberta
has given her the push she needs. With new-found courage, Ricky confronts Elizabeth, who says that Courtney is contented where he is and
that Court's happiness should be Ricky's priority. Ricky agrees, but
bravely replies that she is the one to keep him happy. She adds, "Either
that or I don't belong at all." For the first time in her life, Elizabeth
has fought and lost. She tells Ricky, "Do as you like."

In the spring of 1920, Ricky and Courtney move into an
apartment. While Court is happy with his home life, he is having
problems at the office. He disagrees with his father on editorial policy.
Matthew has conservative ideas, whereas Court's are more liberal. He
also has a personal problem: he learns that Elsa has married, which for
some reason is a shock to his pride.

Not long after they move into their new home, Ricky becomes
pregnant. Matthew thinks it would be good for her to spend some time
at the house in Bar Harbor, Maine, but a worrisome letter from Beulah,
her mother's maid, prompts Ricky to visit Ohio, where Mrs. Stafford
lives. It does not take long for Ricky to sense that something is wrong.
Beulah will say only that Mrs. Stafford has seemed detached since her
son, Dave, died.

That summer, with Elizabeth in Maine, Matthew overseas, and
Ricky not yet home from Ohio, Courtney is left alone in New York.
One afternoon, he runs into Emmy Baldwin, an old friend. He invites
her to dinner and later she asks him to her apartment. He spends the
night with her. A day or two later, Ricky returns from Ohio and with a
sense of guilt Courtney meets her at the station.

In September, Matthew comes back from abroad. He has
learned about Elsa von Wagner and wonders if Court is committed to
her, but Court assures him that he has no obligations there. Meanwhile, the battle about conservative and liberal books goes on between
Matthew and Courtney, although Court's ideas have become more conservative now that he has a son, Jeffrey. America is now entering the
decade of the roaring twenties. Ricky cares for her baby while a restless Courtney pursues an active night life. Ricky realizes that the relationship with her husband is changing. The next summer Ricky takes
the baby to Bar Harbor, while Court stays in New York. With Emmy
now a reader for the firm, Court is more involved with her than ever.
But he warns Emmy that the situation must end when Ricky returns.
Meanwhile, Ricky, who is pregnant with their second child, is very ill,

and the doctor tells Courtney she should have no more. The baby is a girl they name Peggy.

In May, Ricky receives another letter from Beulah saying that Mrs. Stafford has little money and is thinking of moving. Ricky goes home, and again her mother and Beulah evade her questions. Armed with information about her mother's large withdrawals of money from the bank, Ricky asks what is going on, but Mrs. Stafford tells Ricky it is not her concern.

Finally, Beulah decides it is time to tell Ricky the whole story. Annie Stewart, a farm girl, has a son, Pete, who she claims is Dave's. Before Dave went off to war, Jake, Annie's father, insisted that he marry his daughter. Since then, Mrs. Stafford has been blackmailed to keep the matter quiet. Now Ricky knows where Dave's insurance money is going—to Annie. She informs Jake Stewart that his blackmail days have ended: all the money is gone.

Just before Ricky returns home, Sheila Truesdale, who is now in the decorating business, finds a house for Court, and with his mother's approval, he decides to buy it. Ricky is upset to hear the news, because with Court now committed to a house and mortgage, she cannot help her mother financially. She says nothing to him, but instead tells Matthew, who lends his support so that Mrs. Stafford will not have to move.

Early that summer, Courtney receives a letter from Professor von Wagner, in which he mentions that Elsa's son, Otto, is growing rapidly. Court responds to the letter and then gives it no further thought.

Ricky has become reconciled to the idea of a new house. But when she asks Court about the cost, he evades the issue. Worse still, Elizabeth seems to be taking over the house, injecting her ideas and even paying for certain items. Disturbed by this intervention, Ricky confronts Elizabeth, who tries to rectify the problem by showing Ricky the plans. Meanwhile, Courtney and Matthew continue to disagree about the firm's policy. Then one day Court, without mentioning it to Matthew, returns author Anne Lockwood's manuscript to her, with a letter stating that the story is not suited to the taste of the times. When Matthew learns that Courtney and Mather agreed with Emmy Baldwin on the manuscript rejection, he is furious, as Lockwood's books have sold well. Consequently, Emmy is fired. Matthew buys Anne's book, which was accepted by another publisher, and finds he enjoys it. He thinks, "Perhaps it was dated. If so, he was dated too. Maybe Courtney was right, and that damned Baldwin woman too. Anne was writing about a static world, a peaceful world, safe and secure. Not one which had vanished with the war."

A letter arrives from Beulah stating that Annie has gone off and Mrs. Stafford has the care of little Pete. Ricky sends her a check and that evening tells Courtney about Matthew helping out. Although

Court is angry that she did not come to him for the money, he decides to tell Emmy he can no longer pay her rent. This will enable him to send Ricky's mother $100 a month. Just before moving day, Ricky comes upon Courtney's old uniforms in a trunk. In one of the pockets, she finds a letter from Elsa intimating that she was about to have his child. Now everything is clear to Ricky: the change in Court's letters and her uneasiness when he came home from Germany. Ricky hides the note in her jewel case. That night, Courtney discovers the letter. He confesses his relationship with Elsa but assures her there is no child. Ricky finally concludes his escapade was a substitute for the time they never had together because he entered the service so soon after they were married.

Meanwhile Elizabeth, who had sold some of her government bonds to furnish her son's house, has told Courtney she wants to sell the rest and play the stock market with the money. Courtney agrees to help and soon Elizabeth is enjoying her new-found wealth. So excited is she that she refuses to heed Courtney's warnings that the market will not continue its upward trend forever.

By the spring of 1929, Matthew is quite certain that Elizabeth is playing the stock market. When he learns she has sold all her government bonds, he is dismayed. Leaving Courtney in New York, Matthew goes to Maine, where the family members are spending the summer as usual. A feared boating mishap involving his grandchildren is the basis for repeated attempts to call Courtney, but he cannot be found. Of course, Courtney is spending the night at Emmy's place. On his return the next morning, he learns about the children, who are safe after all, and also discovers that his father is ill. That night Court takes the train to Maine and finds Matthew seriously afflicted with pneumonia. Eventually Matthew's health improves, but Ricky and Court's relationship does not. Ricky is justifiably suspicious because he could not be found the night they tried to call him about Peggy and Jeff.

Despite—or perhaps because of—the friction between them, Ricky begins leaving the responsibility of the children to Courtney during his stay in Maine. Her intention is for him to become acquainted with them and to realize what he might have lost. The day Courtney leaves for New York, Ricky informs him that she always knows when he is lying and will not take him back from another woman. In the fall, however, when Elizabeth and Ricky return home, she and Court attempt a reconciliation.

But now another event intervenes. It is October 1929. When Elizabeth decides to take her money out of the market, it is too late: the market crashes and she loses everything. Typically self-centered, she wonders, "How could they do such a thing to me?" She places the blame for her losses on everyone but herself. Not only must the New York and Bar Harbor houses be put up for sale, but Court and Ricky's house has to be mortgaged to help Elizabeth. Roberta finds an apartment for Matthew and Elizabeth; on the day they move, Elizabeth says to the peacock, a family heirloom, "You brought us bad luck after all, Fanny." Even the peacock does not escape Elizabeth's resentment at losing her money.

In the summer of 1931, Ricky and the children go to visit her mother, who is very ill. One evening, Annie Stewart unexpectedly shows up. She has come for Pete. Playing on his sympathy, she convinces Pete to go away with her. When Mrs. Stafford learns of this, she collapses and dies.

In the meantime, Courtney has traveled to Europe on business. Having found the book business discouraging in London and Paris, Courtney flies to Berlin, where he goes to see Professor von Wagner. When the professor shows him a picture of Elsa and Otto, Courtney is shocked at the boy's resemblance to Jeff. That the child is his has been a well-kept secret. He remembers a saying that "old sins left long shadows." He knew now that they did.

Back at home, Elizabeth's health is failing, but she will not see a doctor. So concerned are Court and Matthew about their business that they do not notice how weak she is. By the fall of 1935 Elizabeth is in constant pain and failing quickly. Aware that she does not have much longer to live, she apologizes to Ricky for the way she has behaved toward her. Matthew promises Elizabeth he will not let her live too long in pain; so when she cannot stand it anymore, at her request he reluctantly ends her suffering with a hypodermic.

Elizabeth may be dead but Courtney finds that his past is not. Adele, a member of Courtney's staff, puts a picture of Otto Reiff on his desk. Trying to appear nonchalant, he tosses the photo into his desk drawer. Later when he looks for it, the photo is gone.

In 1938, war clouds are gathering over Europe, and Roberta returns to England, where she feels she can be helpful. The war still does not seem close to America. But by 1939, the United States knows it must get involved.

Jeff, a young man now, feels it is his duty to enlist. He purposely causes trouble at school and is expelled so that he can join the Army Air Corps. Now both he and cousin Pete are in the service. In the winter of 1933 Jay Burton, the Stafford family lawyer, had found Pete and sent him to a military school. Pete subsequently enlisted in the Air Corps. When the news of Pearl Harbor comes over the radio, Court and Ricky know Jeff will have to go. Even Peggy plans to enlist. One by one the boys in the office leave for the service. Courtney carries on with the business with little assistance, but the manuscripts are changing. Instead of "romantic treatment of war" as in World War I, the books are now "hard, factual, and uncompromising."

When Courtney hears the Germans have again bombed London, he asks Adele if she knows what has become of the photograph of

Otto. Adele suspects that Emmy may have taken it. When she confronts Emmy about the photo, her suspicions are confirmed and she retrieves it from her. Because Adele is anxious to tell Courtney that she has found the photo, she takes it to his home, but he is out; so she gives it to Ricky who is shocked at the resemblance to her son, Jeff. Ricky suggests that she return the photo to Courtney's desk drawer and tell him she found it. Court comes upon it later and tears it up.

But the war demands much of their attention. With Courtney now an air raid warden and Ricky a driver for the American Women's Voluntary Services, they are too busy to discuss what is happening to their relationship. Matthew the peacemaker, ever aware of the rift between them, warns Court that he may be losing his wife. Then he tells Ricky that if Courtney did a foolish thing, it happened a long time ago and is over now. She agrees and promises she will not leave him. Not long after their talk, Matthew dies. When Ricky tells Courtney she will miss Matthew, he assures her that she still has her husband.

In the spring of 1943, Jeff expects to be flying out soon and decides to tell his parents about Audrey, a girl he is thinking of marrying. Courtney cautions him about leaving a wife behind during war time, but admits he did the same. Soon after Jeff and Audrey are married, Jeff sails for England.

Late in 1943, Jeffrey is reported missing. Ricky says, "The sins of the fathers, Court." When asked what she means, she says, "Suppose it was your German son who shot him down?" Now he is sure she knows about Otto. Meanwhile, the Allied forces continue to push forward against the German army. By New Year's Day, the Allied planes make their last offensive and the enemy starts to fall. The end of the war is near, but Court and Ricky have no news of Jeff. Neither have they heard from Peggy, who has married a sergeant in the Army Air Force, for some time.

One day in 1945 when Ricky returns from the park, a young man in uniform is standing on the sidewalk, looking up at the number on the house. She asks if he has news of Jeff. No, he responds, he is her son-in-law, Terry Shane, and has just returned from the Pacific. He does not know of Peggy's whereabouts, either. On Saturday morning when Court goes to the office, he finds an envelope from Switzerland in the mail. In it is a photo of a grave with a wooden cross bearing the insignia of an airman. "Otto" is written on the back. That evening, Courtney tells Ricky that Otto, who was a Nazi, is dead; since Court never was a real father to him, they cannot grieve over the boy. She understands and now the barrier between them is almost down.

Fall of 1945: Ricky now loves the house she once hated so much. Staying with them is Audrey, who is expecting the arrival of Jeff, and Peggy will be home soon. Remembering how frightened she was when she first came to live with Elizabeth and Matthew, Ricky is determined to make her daughter-in-law comfortable. It has been three years since Jeff and Audrey have seen each other, and Audrey is worried that he may have forgotten her. Ricky eases her fears by telling her that she, too, was afraid when Court returned. When Audrey says she had no idea that Ricky was afraid of anything, Ricky replies, "My dear, my whole life has been one fear after another. And I'd been married in such a hurry. I was sure Court wouldn't love me when he came back. I pretty nearly lost him too." She advises Audrey to let Jeff know as soon as she sees him that she loves him. Now Ricky has done what she knows is right and feels sure Audrey will not make the same mistake she did.

When at last Jeff arrives, Ricky and Court share a moment of remembering how different it was when Court came home. That evening, Jeff tells Court about a French girl with whom he became involved and recalls that circumstances were pretty much the same as with Court and his German girl. He plans to tell Audrey. Court is uncertain about this plan, but Jeff responds, "Better now than later, Dad."

Next, Jeff inquires about the publishing business and much to Court's relief, he says, "Well, I guess we'll manage. I see we have a new Lockwood." Court tells his son he will be proud to have him in the family firm, and looks ahead to the future. He thinks, "[We will] publish honest books...follow Matthew's example of integrity and essential simplicity. And Americanism."

CONFLICTS

Although the historical events in this novel—World War I, the depression, and World War II—outweigh the characters' personal problems, their own battles may seem like war to them as they struggle with resentment, fear, and jealousy.

As is evident from the following, resentment heads the list of conflicts among the characters:

1). **Elizabeth**, jealous of Ricky, resents the war for having ruined plans for her son and herself, not to mention Courtney's marriage and the loss of money in the stock market.
2). **Matthew** resents society's effect on book publishing.
3). **Ricky**, jealous of Courtney's other woman and his son, Otto, resents living in the Wayne house, Courtney's domestic pattern, and Elizabeth's interference in her life.
4). **Courtney** resents the critics' poor reviews of any of his published books.
5). **Emmy**, jealous of Ricky, resents Courtney's marriage to her.
6). **Mrs. Stafford**, fearful that people might learn about Dave, Annie, and son Pete, resents that her son was not buried beside

his father and that Ricky found out about Dave's son. She also revolts against Ricky and society in general.

Of all the characters, Mrs. Stafford has more than her share of resentments. Although she expresses bitterness in some ways, her resentful silence in other ways is probably more upsetting to herself than to her family. She is in ill health, and because she remains silent about her problems, not allowing anyone to help her, she ages rapidly. She allows her bitterness to poison her outlook and separate her from the very people who could offer her comfort.

THEMES

When a person exerts undue influence over another, we may examine motives and conclude that he or she means well. But as Matthew's sister, Roberta, says, "The world is full of people who mean well and destroy whatever they touch." In a similar manner, Elizabeth works hard at trying to dominate Ricky's life, intending to insure a good life for her son. Ricky fights against her interference and in the end Elizabeth apologizes for her behavior. She has meant well but not always done well.

Another strong thematic element in the novel involves a world widely affected by change. The time span of twenty-five years encompasses two world wars and a depression, and Rinehart reflects the changes in the world at large in the looking glass of Wayne Publishing. The conflicts surrounding Matthew's insistence on the "old-fashioned" ways of story telling and Courtney's desire for more "modern" subjects clearly represent changes in the tastes of society at large. The simpler times of the pre-World War I era are gone, replaced by a world confronted with problems on a global scale.

Still, Courtney discovers that Matthew is right in some respects: in publishing, as in life, there are some verities worth keeping, and the return to writer Anne Lockwood at the end of the novel indicates that the publishing house—and perhaps the world—may be rediscovering the value of the lessons of history.

Rinehart also deals in this novel with the difficulty in breaking down strong social differences. Once again the class boundaries are clearly drawn. A snobbish person concerned with wealth and status, Elizabeth is intolerant of Ricky but eventually admits that she, like Ricky, was raised "very simply." In Elizabeth's estimation, Ricky is from the wrong side of the tracks. Elizabeth does not say this in so many words, but the implication is strong. She is dismayed over her son's marriage and does little to support its success. Clearly, she seems to think that Courtney "could've done better," a belief that colors her relationship with both Ricky and her son.

NARRATIVE SUSPENSE

A Light in the Window, built around two World Wars and The Depression, is obviously not the typical Rinehart "whodunit," but instead an extended study of the lives of a family over the course of two decades. The novel contains little humor, a common component of Rinehart's stories. The last of Rinehart's serious novels, this book is of simple narrative structure even though it contains many characters.

Although several people die, Rinehart does not go into lengthy detail about the events. As difficult as it may be, her characters accept the loss of their loved ones and get on with living. The approach is realistic, which is quite typical for a writer like Rinehart, who utilizes personal experiences in her fiction. Her characters speak in a manner natural to place and situation; this helps solidify the book's realism. When Courtney visits Professor Hans von Wagner in Germany, for example, the professor's wife greets him in German, while von Wagner answers Courtney's questions "in quite good if accented English."

SYMBOLISM

Perhaps the most outstanding visible representation of status for Elizabeth is the house she and Matthew bought and rebuilt. Looking at it from the outside, she views it as a symbol of her keen mind and the success of her husband. When indoors, she experiences a "quieting effect." To her the entire house is a miracle.

The reception room, which Elizabeth refers to as "Mama's parlor," suggests the dead past—this is where she sits when she feels she cannot face the future. In this room is a stuffed peacock named Fanny because its tail is open like a fan. Some consider the peacock bad luck, but for Elizabeth the bird is more than that: she speaks to it in a prayerful way, as one might to an idol. Perhaps Elizabeth's reverence for the bird is grounded in ancient tradition. As early as 1200 B.C., peacock feathers were used by the Egyptians in making umbrellas and fans. It was deemed a great honor to be invited to stand in the shade of an umbrella belonging to nobility, the shade being a symbol of the king's protection. Elizabeth, for whom high rank is important, may have felt its representation in Fanny.

THE MODERN GOTHIC

In 1960 Donald A. Wollheim and Evelyn Grippo of Ace Books created the modern gothic paperback genre by publishing several romantic suspense novels with a distinct cover package that featured a beautiful woman running in fear away from a dark house or castle. In each case just one light was lit on one of the upper floors of the structure. Other paperback companies copied the package, and by 1970 hundreds of gothics, original and reprint, were being published annually. The genre had virtually died by 1980. "The light in the window"—and the type of women's mystery story so popularized by Mary Roberts Rinehart—reached their ultimate realization in this paperback category.

X.

THE SWIMMING POOL
(1952)

THE STORY

After the panic of 1929, Lois Maynard and her brother Phil, an unsuccessful lawyer, move from the townhouse in the city to a place called The Birches, so named for a grove of trees not far from the house. What has been the family's summer residence for years has now, of necessity, become their permanent home. It nestles in the hills of a peaceful countryside and was at one time an elegant piece of property. Despite Lois's efforts to restore the place, it looks run down after years of neglect, but nevertheless the isolated house is still an impressive sight.

A swimming pool, then considered by many people to be a distinctive quality, lies near the house. The pool itself has a certain history. Although Lois's father objected to building it, Judith, her mother's favorite offspring, wanted it, and the spoiled child got her way. As the sisters grew, the pool was a popular place, especially for Judith's crowd, mostly college boys, who were heavy drinkers. In those days, the shrubbery by the pool was a good place to discard empty flasks and bottles; now it will prove a perfect spot for prowlers to hide.

A gentleman by the name of Ridgely Chandler, who came from a wealthy, prominent family, fit into Mother's plans perfectly—but not Judith's. He was twenty years older than she, and although he was very much in love with her, she did not love him. Instead, her interests centered on Johnny Shannon, a law student at Columbia, who was falsely accused of murder. Judith was his only alibi. At the time of the killing, she was with him in his room until early morning. When questioned later by Inspector Flaherty, she lied, as did Mother and Dawson, the butler, in order to protect her own reputation. Helga, the family cook, also knew, but was too loyal to say anything. Flaherty, who never felt Shannon was guilty, was murdered one night when attempting to see Dawson to make him tell the truth.

Although Father, a kind, softspoken man, was not told the true story about Judith, he knew she was in some sort of trouble. After a dinner party one evening in January 1930, he went back to his office and shot himself. The reason for this act was unclear. However, he was in financial straits and, it was thought, probably distraught because he could not raise enough money to save his daughter's reputation. Here, Rinehart echoes the frustrations and financial troubles of her own father, who also committed suicide.

As the reader discovers later, Mother, still determined to uphold the family name, asked Ridgely for a large amount of money to stifle adverse publicity about Judith being involved in a car accident. This was a lie: Mother needed the money to pay Dawson, who was blackmailing her for Judith's indiscretion with Shannon. Not long after Father's death, Judith was persuaded to marry Ridgely.

Now, twenty years later, the oldest sister, Anne, comes to visit Lois at The Birches and tells her that Judith has been acting strangely and is being treated by Dr. Townsend, a Park Avenue psychiatrist. Anne says Judith is planning to divorce her husband, which means that Lois is tied to a promise she made to her mother before she died; she pledged to take care of Judith if ever she should need it.

A day or two later Ridgely is seen driving up. He, too, apparently is concerned with his wife's strange behavior. He tells Lois that for some reason Judith is frightened and he asks Lois to spy on her. When she refuses, he says she is indebted to him because he paid her way through college. So Lois is trapped into accompanying Judith on a trip the latter is planning to Reno.

When Lois meets Judith in New York for the journey West, Judith looks different, as though she is trying to disguise herself. She eyes the crowd feverishly, not relaxing until they are on the train, but even then she stays in her room and berth for most of the trip. In Reno, she seems more like her old self, enjoying the attention of men who, as always, flock around her.

As the sisters are preparing to return to the east coast, Judith announces that once she gets there she plans to stay at The Birches for a while. Lois and Anne are against the idea, but Judith holds firm. As she and Lois board the train for the East, Judith is smiling, but as it moves out, leaving a group of waving men admirers, Judith suddenly feels faint. Terrence O'Brien of the New York Police Department, who just "happens" to be on board, helps Lois take her sister to her drawing room. Had one of the faces in the crowd upset her? Nothing seemed amiss. One or two taxis drove up and that was about all. Judith locks herself in her room until they are nearing New York.

Helga and Jennie, the servants, are at The Birches when Lois and Judith arrive and from the look on Helga's face, Lois knows there will be trouble. Judith takes over Mother's room, where for her entire visit, she will remain, except for meals and for walks at night dressed in a dark cape. She has all her jewels with her and wants her doors locked and the windows nailed shut. Lois asks why she is afraid and what she has done wrong, but Judith denies any wrong doing: she is simply taking precautions.

One evening, when Jennie is sitting on the bench by the pool, a dark figure suddenly appears and points a gun at her. Screaming, she runs back to the house, where she tells Phil that the stranger said he had to talk to her and that she knew why. Later, Lois meets officer O'Brien again. He wants to rent the cottage by her place on the pretext of planting seeds and owning a few chickens; but his main reason is to protect Judith. He knows something. After O'Brien is well settled, the real mystery begins to take shape.

One hot night Bill, Anne's son, who is also staying at The Birches, awakens Lois. He had dived into the pool on top of the body of a woman. Judith arrives soon after, takes one look and faints. The police believe it is murder, that the unidentified woman was struck on the head and then thrown into the pool. A few days later, around eleven o'clock in the evening, Lois sees someone toss a rock through Judith's window. Realizing that Judith is very frightened because she may in fact be in danger, Lois decides to talk with officer O'Brien. At midnight she dresses in Judith's black cape and as she is walking rapidly past the pool, a man grabs her; upon discovering she is not Judith, he playfully tosses her into the water.

One crime follows another: Bill is hit over the head; O'Brien is shot; and Lois is knocked down by an intruder hiding in the hall by Judith's door. Unstable and unable to bear the pressure of these events, Judith attempts suicide, but is unsuccessful. By now she feels even more threatened, and tries to book overseas passage on the *Queen Mary*. The passage is fully booked, but later a man telephones to say there has been a cancellation and a car is being sent to take her to the ship. A large black car arrives; Judith gets in, puts her jewel case on her lap, waves goodbye to Lois, and is gone.

The next morning the car is found overturned: the driver has been shot and killed and Judith has disappeared, along with the jewel case she had with her. A search ensues. She is found unconscious but alive, and is taken to the hospital. Little by little information comes to light. The driver was Johnny Shannon. Because of the lie Judith had told twenty years before, she was primarily responsible for his being in prison. Then he was released. In Reno she saw him driving a taxi (he also saw her and there was bitterness and hatred in his face), and from then on she was terrified that he would try to contact her. She was right. After being shut away for twenty years, he had become obsessed with the idea of clearing his name, and Judith was his only hope.

Officer O'Brien has felt for some time that there was a clever mind operating behind many of the strange happenings. He lays a trap and apprehends Judith's estranged husband, Ridgely Chandler, who has murdered three people: Flaherty; Kate Henry, the woman found in the pool; and Shannon.

The Birches is no longer a peaceful place. After all that has happened, Lois and Phil do not want to stay there. It is sold to a couple with young children, one of whom promptly tumbles into the pool; the new owner says to his wife, "I'm afraid it will have to go, my dear." And the sluice gates are opened. Much later, after many appeals, Ridgely Chandler is convicted of Shannon's murder. He bought Judith to save her reputation and incidentally send Shannon to prison. However, Lois tells Anne, "He meant to marry her. He paid the $50,000 to save his family name. Not ours." A romance that has blossomed throughout the story ends happily with Lois marrying O'Brien.

CHARACTERS

Judith is well named, for she makes an interesting comparison to her namesake in the Apocrypha. Both Judiths are captivating beauties who have a profound effect on other characters, but those effects are different indeed. The biblical Judith is respected for her wisdom and the truth she speaks, while Rinehart's is deceitful and evasive. The first Judith takes personal risks; the second locks herself away in desperate fear, choosing The Birches as a place of safety rather than facing danger. Finally, the crimes that each commits are different: one is done in the name of righteousness and the other for selfish reasons. Although Judith Chandler does not commit murder—the biblical Judith decapitates a man—her initial lie sets the stage for crimes of varying degrees of seriousness.

Lois, through whose eyes the story is told with occasional flashbacks, is the youngest of the four Maynard children, but a big disappointment to her mother. She was the ugly duckling: her hair was black and straight, her eyes gray, and she had one or two teeth missing. In her early days she was what one might label a tomboy. Lois has written one or two books, and at present is working on a detective story.

Anne, the oldest daughter, is married to Martin Harrison, an unsuccessful architect. She is practical, solidly built, and completely domestic. Martin and Anne have two children, Bill and Martha.

Mr. and Mrs. Maynard, referred to in the novel as Mother and Father, are mentioned only in flashbacks, since neither is living at the time the story takes place. Their influence is a strong presence, however, especially in light of a series of events that occurred some years before the story actually starts.

A large, domineering woman, Mother was very much aware of her wealth and place in society. Her supreme hope was that Judith would make a good marriage and restore the family fortunes. For that to happen, she would have attempted anything but murder.

Mystery surrounds not only the circumstances, but the characters as well. The cast is large and the reader never feels close to, nor truly understands, any one of them. Confusion arises in this respect involving changes in names, either through the use of an alias or by marriage. For example, Johnny Shannon spent some time in Reno as a taxi driver under the name of Alec Morrison. Katherine Selina Benjamin, once known as Kate Henry (the woman found in the pool), used the name Selina Benjamin after she married Arthur Dawson, the butler, who changed his name to Walter Benjamin.

CONFLICTS

The novel becomes even more complicated through a variety of conflicts, all of which must be resolved by the end. Judith is the center of conflict, plagued as she is by personal turmoil, guilty conscience, egocentricity, and hypersensitivity. Nobody at The Birches is happy to have her there. From the very first day she arrives until the place is sold, problems arise: Phil becomes irritable, Lois's work suffers, and the servants are difficult to manage. After divorcing Chandler, her whole lifestyle changes. Where for twenty years she had led a very visible life of good times and gaiety, now she remains locked in her room and seldom goes anywhere. Consequently, her presence at The Birches combined with the tragedies and strange occurrences that seem to accompany her, puts the entire household in a turmoil.

Judith is filled with internal conflicts which are also reflected in her personal relationships. As sisters, Anne and Judith were never compatible. Now Anne is especially resentful, since she feels that Judith, who has had everything a person could want, seems to have thrown it all away. Similarly, her brother, Phil, gave up trying to understand Judith years ago. He says that even as a child, she made no sense to him. He cares very little for her and resents her being at The Birches.

As for Lois, she was envious of Judith's beauty and also her marriage, with all the money and glamor associated with it. Lois never commanded everyone's attention as did Judith. And finally, she was resentful of the fact that Judith usually had her own way in every respect.

Of all the characters in the story, Johnny Shannon may have been the one most deeply affected by Judith's struggles with herself. He had twenty years in prison to develop an obsession concerning Judith, that of clearing his name, and may have become somewhat abnormal in his thinking toward her. That Judith reacts so violently to his return is an indication of the depth of her guilt over her lie, an emotion matched only by Johnny Shannon's anger over the injustice she perpetrated.

THEMES

The novel is well-constructed, with every piece eventually falling into place. The central theme, "the sins of the fathers are visited on the children," is brought out early in the book and then expanded upon. In this case, the sins of the mothers are involved, too. Mother's pride was all too embracing to allow either herself or Judith to admit the truth that would have kept an innocent man out of prison. Over the span of twenty years, one "sin" sets up an entire series of incidents: divorce, shootings, deaths (including one suicide and one failed attempt), bribery, blackmail, and mistrust among family members. Eventually, the characters "pay" for their misdeeds, but only after innocent people are injured and lives ruined. In the end, perhaps, certain of the characters have learned a difficult lesson. As Phil observes, "Maybe we are better now than we were then...there's not so much pride of the wrong sort, of money or place, or social position. Mother was of her world, but her world has gone kaput."

Another theme in this novel is the power of emotion to wreak havoc in our lives. Judith, for example, suffers from a guilty conscience, which can make a person behave in an abnormal manner, is almost impossible to run away from, and seldom accepts treatment. Judith lives out the torture of a stained conscience, which drives her to near insanity. She even attempts self-destruction.

Ridgely Chandler is equally spiteful because Judith hated him; he could not make her love him, and he could never forgive that. He could only "buy" her affection, a kind of emotional blackmail that may not be unlawful but nonetheless immoral.

Fear, real or imaginary, is also difficult to cope with. The mind can take only so much pressure, from the outside or self-inflicted, and then it reaches a breaking point. Judith is obsessed by her fears, both of having her indiscretion with Shannon discovered and later of his revenge. Fear comes to be the driving force in her life. Dr. Townsend sums it up when he says,

> "I suppose all of us are capable of [murder], more or
> less. Greed, envy, jealousy, rage, fear, self-protec-
> tion, or sheer desperation—who knows what the hu-
> man animal will do? And, of course, there is always
> what we call original sin. Whatever it is it may be the
> matter of a momentary impulse or the result of a long
> train of unconscious preparation. But we do kill."

Narrative Suspense

Rinehart uses many methods to hold the reader's attention, among them a keen awareness of when to discontinue a certain subject. The author sometimes accomplishes this closure through a character's remark, as, for example, Lois says, "Perhaps I am spending too much time on that interval, before our real mystery begins to develop." This conciousness of narrative movement is a Rinehart signature; she moves the plot along just when she needs to do so. To accomplish the movement, Rinehart sprinkles the occasional clue to stimulate the reader, and at those moments one gets the feeling the mystery will be easy to solve long before the novel ends. But Rinehart is not one for easy solutions: the actual story is too well hidden.

Certain sentences, often at chapter endings, foreshadow events and tease the reader even more. For example, when musing about Judith, Lois says, "She was always afraid of the water. Perhaps that excuses her for what happened years later." In the same way, Rinehart tantalizes as another chapter closes: "But that faint was definitely not psychopathic. She *was* terrified, although it was only after long months of what I can only call travail that we learned the reason for it." Foreshadowing is obvious when Lois thinks, "I daresay any train east from that Nevada city carries its own load of drama, but I had no idea it was carrying ours." In this way, Rinehart injects energy and movement into the narrative, speeding it along.

Technique

The Swimming Pool is a complex mystery romance loaded with sometimes confusing flashbacks, a technique Rinehart may have chosen to mislead readers and increase the richness of the mystery. On a superficial level, the novel is a taut, spine-tingling entertainment, a rewarding read. On a deeper level, however, the novel is more complicated than it appears. Some of the confusion can be eliminated by listing the flashbacks, which occur throughout the book and which turn the normal narrative line into a zig-zag. Keeping abreast of Rinehart's time shifts is essential in discerning a pattern that leads to the solution of the mystery. Rinehart has, in short, disguised some of the puzzle pieces here by cloaking them in the fabric of time. The result is a well-tailored story.

In *The Swimming Pool* one hint appears in the first chapter, for example, when Lois is reliving the past and thinks, "Apparently no Chandler ever broke the law." The irony of the statement is heightened when it is connected to Lois's memories of the days of Prohibition: at the time, she doubted that Ridgely joined the younger boys in their surreptitious drinking sprees. The appearance of propriety is strengthened by the passage of time. Lois will learn, however, that appearances can be deceiving and that Ridgely is far from innocent.

Many other references to the Chandlers increase this misapprehension: "The Chandlers can do no wrong"; "The Chandlers don't do things like that"; "He was a gentleman and a Chandler." Rinehart maintains the pretext in her description of an item in a New York newspaper. Judith is suspected of killing Johnny Shannon, but "so far there has been no arrest. The police move slowly when any member of a highly respected family is involved. And both the Chandlers and the Maynards have always stood for the best in the city. It is indicative of this that her ex-husband, Ridgely Chandler, is standing by Judith in this trying time."

Ridgely always appears on the scene after a killing and asks many questions. He even suggests that Judith murdered Johnny Shannon and if found guilty, would no doubt be handed a light sentence. Furthermore, if necessary, they could say she had been of unsound mind for quite a while and he would be willing to testify to the fact. These are but a few of the clues that point away from Chandler. Rinehart so cleverly casts suspicion on her characters that Chandler seems the least likely culprit.

SYMBOLISM

One of several ways Rinehart enriches this novel is through the use of symbols that augment an understanding of both the characters' motivations and the puzzling situations they face. The novel's title suggests the significance of that item as central symbol in the book. The swimming pool at The Birches is a visible representation of the invisible, a constant reminder of the many happy hours spent there in the past; however, as time goes on, the pool becomes a harbinger of impending doom. Psychologists sometimes refer to what they call the "evil eye syndrome," a phenomenon which has existed in every society and which can be characterized as a general fear of catastrophe underlying a period of success and rejoicing. Certainly the pool signifies such a state, as does the shrubbery, with depths that can be equally welcoming and threatening, something that is both shield and hiding place, another sign of abiding danger.

Another symbol is Judith's cape. Whenever she goes for a walk at night, she wears the long black cape for concealment. She is trying to hide, just as she tries to hide behind weak disguises when she has seen Shannon.

The jewel case she keeps in her room is another ploy; it is an excuse for locked doors and nailed windows, but it also implies vanity, greed, and selfishness.

When Lois visits Selina Benjamin's cottage, she sees there a more traditional symbol—a black cat sitting in the window. The curtains around it are badly torn. Figuratively, the black cat has crossed the paths of several people in the novel, whose lives are in tatters from deaths, shootings, thefts, bribery, blackmail, and lies. The portent of bad luck proves alarmingly accurate.

The Laszlo portrait of Mother, often scrutinized by Chandler and members of the Maynard family, is a symbol of the grandeur of the past. Mother looks down from the wall almost regally, and in fact, her influence still rules the family. As befits a queen, in the painting Mother is wearing the pearls and diamond bracelets she was never without, physical manifestations of her high power and rank.

XI.

CONCLUSION

Mary Roberts Rinehart once remarked, "I am constantly being asked why I have chosen to write so many books about crime. The answer is, quite frankly, that I do not know." Perhaps the fact that her first book, *The Circular Staircase*, received such positive reviews influenced her choice of genre and subject in ensuing works. Stating emphatically that she was not a writer of detective books but of novels, she added, "One might even say that each one is really two novels, one of which is the story I tell the reader, and the other the buried story I know and let slip now and then into a clue to whet the reader's interest." For Rinehart, writing was pleasurable, but "the hardest work in the world."

When working, she led a very disciplined lifestyle. Words inspired her; she wrote rapidly, her mind filled with ideas. Her plots, while appropriate to novels that deal with crime, transcend the mere puzzle aspect of the traditional mystery. In a world peopled with interesting, varied characters, driven by believable motivations, Rinehart expressed her concern with the disastrous effects of crime on everyone. She entertains, but she also gives the reader much to think about beyond the accustomed satisfactions of the genre.

To develop her novels, Rinehart relied upon a simple, tightly constructed, straightforward plot with many of the trappings of the conventional thriller-detective story—particularly the death by violence of innocent victims, an emphasis on dialogue and action, and a limited setting. There is a puzzle, but under the puzzle there is a murder—the ultimate crime against humanity.

Rinehart wrote most easily when her narrator was a woman. Drawing upon her life's experiences made this a natural choice of viewpoint, allowing her to create in her characters recognizable human beings whose reations are real. Confronted as they are with dilemmas of all sorts, they draw upon their considerable innate resources to unravel the mystery or solve the problem, much as Rinehart did in her own life. Although the central crime is violent and brutal, the harshness is tempered by romance and humor, as well as a happy ending which she cleverly interweaves for balance. Her theme, as in most mystery fiction, is the juxtaposition of stability played against instability, and stability finally wins.

In all, Rinehart wrote fifty books—beginning with *The Circular Staircase* (1908) and ending with *The Swimming Pool* (1952). In between, she wrote seven plays and countless stories and essays. Although plagued by many health problems, she maintained an optimistic outlook and completed successful careers as a mother and novelist. Having survived three difficult pregnancies, heart attacks, diphtheria, and several surgeries, at age eighty-two, she suffered yet another heart attack from which she died on September 22nd, 1958.

At the time of her death, more than ten million copies of her books had been sold. Whether or not Mary Roberts Rinehart realized the contribution she made to the literary world matters little; her tenacity brought joy not only to herself and her family, but to all her readers, whom she wanted to please. She continues to be one of the most popular mystery writers known today.

SELECTIVE BIBLIOGRAPHY

PRIMARY SOURCES

The Circular Staircase. Indianapolis: Bobbs-Merrill Co., 1908.
The Case of Jennie Brice. Indianapolis: Bobbs-Merrill Co., 1913.
The Red Lamp. New York: Geo. M. Doran, 1925.
Lost Ecstasy. New York: Geo. M. Doran, 1927.
The Door. New York: Farrar & Rinehart, 1930.
The Great Mistake. New York: Farrar & Rinehart, 1940.
The Haunted Lady. New York: Farrar & Rinehart, 1942.
The Yellow Room. New York: Farrar & Rinehart, 1945.
A Light in the Window. New York: Rinehart & Co., 1948.
The Swimming Pool. New York: Rinehart & Co., 1952.

SECONDARY SOURCES

Barnard, Robert. *A Talent to Deceive.* New York: The Mysterious Press, 1987.
Bletzer, June G. *The Donning International Encyclopedic Psychic Dictionary.* Norfolk, VA: Donning, 1986.
Cirlot, J. C. *A Dictionary of Symbols.* New York: Philosophical Library, 1971.
Cohn, Jan. *Improbable Fiction: The Life of Mary Roberts Rinehart.* Pittsburgh: University of Pittsburgh Press, 1980.
Kunitz, Stanley J. and Howard Haycraft, eds. *Twentieth-Century Authors: A Biographical Dictionary of Modern Literature.* New York: H. W. Wilson Co., 1942. Second Edition 1955.
Magill, Frank N., ed. *Masterpieces of World Literature.* New York: Harper & Row, 1949. Second Edition 1955, Third Edition 1969.
Norville, Barbara. *Writing the Modern Mystery.* Cincinnati: Writer's Digest Books, 1986.
Panati, Charles. *Extraordinary Origins of Everyday Things.* New York: Harper & Row, 1987.
Rinehart, Mary Roberts. *Crime Book.* New York, Toronto: Rinehart, 1921.
Rinehart, Mary Roberts. *My Story.* Chicago: Cadmus Books, E. M. Hale, 1931.

Sicherman, Barbara and Carol Hurd Green, *et. al.*, eds. *Notable American Women: The Modern Period: A Biographical Dictionary.* Cambridge, MA: Harvard University Press, 1980.

Stevenson, Robert Louis. *The Strange Case of Dr. Jekyll and Mr. Hyde.* London: Longmans, Green, 1886.

Stoker, Bram. *Dracula.* New York: Dell, 1965.

Stowe, Harriet Beecher. *Uncle Tom's Cabin.* Boston: J. P. Jewett, 1852.

Trawick, Buckner B. *The Bible as Literature.* New York: Barnes & Noble, 1970.

Van Doren, Charles, ed. *Webster's American Biographies.* Springfield, MA: G. & C. Merriam, 1974.

INDEX

TITLE INDEX
Works by Mary Roberts Rinehart

SUBJECT INDEX

Many of the recurring clues, symbols, themes and plot devices listed here were closely associated with, and became almost signatures of, Rinehart's work.

PLACE INDEX

Rinehart used similar and recurring locales and sites for her novels,
which frequently were set on an estate or in an old family home, and
reflected the class and social conflicts which were key themes in her
work.

CHARACTER INDEX

*Rinehart used recurring and similar character names, family group-
ings, and occupations for her stories, which often featured dogs (but
in one case a canary!) who played significant roles in the plot devel-
opment. Her female protagonists were normally surrounded by servants and old family retainers, who were usually supportive, but who
could, on occasion, prove treacherous.*

ABOUT THE AUTHOR

FRANCES HELEN BACHELDER was born in Athol, Massachusetts, but grew up in Orange. The daughter of a highly skilled metal cabinet-maker, she worked as a secretary in a local defense plant during World War II. In 1944, she married an officer in the U.S. Navy. After the war, they moved to Amherst, where she attended the University of Massachusetts. During their fourteen-year stay there, two sons were born.

She started piano lessons at age six. From then on, music became a high point in her life. In 1960, the family moved to West Lafayette, Indiana, where she continued her musical pursuits at Purdue University. Their older son left for California in 1969 and received his Ph.D. at the University of Southern California. In 1970, she and her husband and younger son moved to Presque Isle, Maine, and remained there for ten years, before making one last move in 1980, to San Diego, California. Their younger son had left for college in Florida by then.

Until this time, Bachelder had not realized that writing would become such an important part of her life. Her first effort, an essay on the British novelist Barbara Pym entitled "The Importance of Connecting," appeared in *The Life and Work of Barbara Pym* (London: Macmillan; Iowa City, IA: University of Iowa Press, 1987). Another essay, also on Pym, was published in the *St. James Reference Guide to English Literature* (Chicago, London: St. James Press, 1991). A third essay, on Anne Tyler's novels, will be published in a collection of essays on the American novelist.

Along with her literary studies, Bachelder also writes children's poetry and is now completing her first novel.

Printed in the USA
CPSIA information can be obtained
at www.ICGtesting.com
LVHW042321300723
753896LV00008B/191